A THOUSAND KISSES DEEP

Novoneel Chakraborty is the prolific author of fifteen bestselling thriller novels, two e-novellas and one bestselling short-story collection, with his works being translated into multiple Indian languages. Almost all his novels have debuted in the top three Nielsen listings across India and have continued to be in the top positions on various bestseller lists for several months after release.

His Forever series made it to the *Times of India*'s Most Stunning Books of 2017 list, while the Stranger trilogy became a phenomenal hit among young adults, with Amazon tagging it, along with his erotic thriller *Black Suits You*, as their memorable reads of the year. He has sold over 1 million copies and is India's most popular thriller novelist. His twists, dark plots and strong female protagonists have earned him the moniker 'Sidney Sheldon of India'.

The Stranger trilogy, his immensely popular thriller series, has been translated into six Indian languages. The trilogy has also been adapted into a successful web series by Applause Entertainment and Rose Audio Visuals on MX Player, amassing a whopping 500 million-plus views. Other successful adaptations for the screen include *Black Suits You* and the Forever series.

Novoneel has written several hit TV and original web shows for premier channels like MX Player, Sony, Star Plus, Zee and Zee5. He lives and works in Mumbai.

ALSO BY THE SAME AUTHOR

Half Torn Hearts
The Best Couple Ever
Cheaters

FOREVER SERIES
Forever Is a Lie
Forever Is True

THE STRANGER TRILOGY
Marry Me, Stranger
All Yours, Stranger
Forget Me Not, Stranger

EX
How about a Sin Tonight?
Black Suits You
Roses Are Blood Red
Cross Your Heart, Take My Name
Whisper to Me Your Lies

A THOUSAND KISSES DEEP

NOVONEEL CHAKRABORTY

Penguin
metro reads

An imprint of Penguin Random House

PENGUIN METRO READS

USA | Canada | UK | Ireland | Australia
New Zealand | India | South Africa | China

Penguin Metro Reads is part of the Penguin Random House group of companies
whose addresses can be found at global.penguinrandomhouse.com

Published by Penguin Random House India Pvt. Ltd
4th Floor, Capital Tower 1, MG Road,
Gurugram 122 002, Haryana, India

Penguin
Random House
India

First published in Penguin Metro Reads by Penguin Random House India 2022

ISBN 9780143458234

Typeset in Requiem by MAP Systems, Bengaluru, India
Printed at Thomson Press India Ltd, New Delhi

www.penguin.co.in

MIX
Paper
FSC FSC® C010616

For my peace-point, R.

Prologue

He was in his new Mercedes-Maybach. The chauffeur was constantly chirping about how smooth the car was. None of it was falling on Haasil Sinha's ears, who was sitting behind with the photo gallery open on his phone. The photos were of Palki and him. All once-upon-a-time clicks. *Or was it once-upon-a-life?* Haasil wondered. Since morning that day, he had been missing her. Something he had trained his mind not to do for some years now after having called Pallavi's bluff and learnt about Palki's missing body. She was now presumed dead.

Haasil didn't remember Palki's birthday after the devastating accident. It was his best friend Nitin Punjabi who had told him the date much later. And today was the day. He kept looking at their photographs, immersing himself in nostalgia. Their wedding photos, travel pictures, candid moments, all captured in time. It struck him that a camera wasn't a handy thing back then like it is now. You could preserve everyday moments now on your phone. How he wished it was there those years ago. He would have known their own love story in greater detail.

After the exposé of Pallavi, who was only an imposter as far as Haasil was concerned, he used to cut a cake in Palki's name alone on this day. Ordered Palki's favourite flowers, about which he found out from Nitin again, and then lived the day in their fragrance. He continued doing so for a few years. But his present was different. He was someone's husband now. And he couldn't possibly tell his wife that he was missing his ex-wife on her birthday. Not that his wife would mind, but Haasil knew it could possibly give rise to some questions which, he thought, they could do without.

As his car came to a halt at a junction, Haasil casually looked up to see the traffic signal displaying a digital clock on a countdown of 120 seconds. His phone was open to a photo of Palki and him but that changed to a screen flashing a call from his company's CFO. His emotions were protesting but Haasil knew it was important to take the call. And after taking the call, he knew he would soon reach his office in Cyber Hub, Gurugram, and be hurled into yet another work schedule which, by the time it ended, the day would have vanished into oblivion. And he would have to live his present shrugging off the past. Haasil sighed and took the call. As the signal turned green, he felt the car move but in the immediate second after, he felt the jolt of the emergency brake and jerked forward suddenly.

'What are you doing, Ram?' Haasil said, irked. He was still on the call. As Haasil raised his head, his ears didn't register what his chauffeur had said for his eyes had fallen on her. For a second, Haasil thought his mind was playing some trick. He hastily ended the call. By then she had crossed the road and had stepped on to the adjacent footpath. With his car not moving, horns were blaring from behind.

'You drive on,' Haasil instructed and stepped out of the car, cat-quick. Ram found it weird but didn't say anything. Out on the road, Haasil felt there was a surreal feel to it all. *It's her birthday and I actually see her . . . someone who is supposedly dead?* He could feel knots in his stomach. It can't be her for sure and yet . . . Haasil managed to cross the road and reach the footpath. He could still see her in an off-white dress, black footwear and a bag hanging on her shoulder, walking ahead briskly.

As Haasil took big strides to reach her, he found himself in a daze. He could feel an adrenaline rush. He was sure someone would wake him up and inform him it was all a dream. *How could it be her? Or was it Pallavi again?*

It took Haasil half a minute to reach right behind her. She stood by the side of another road, waiting to cross it after the traffic subsided a bit. Haasil came up and stood next to her. He now had a look at her face. He skipped few heartbeats. She was about to cross the road when he said, 'Excuse me.'

She turned to look at Haasil. His reflection was clear on her Ray-Ban Wayfarers. She took them off.

'Yes?' she asked. The voice wasn't Pallavi's, that was the first thing Haasil noticed. And it made his breaths ever shorter. He looked at her with such intensity that it made her uncomfortable.

'Do I know you?' she asked.

Does she know him? They were each other's intimate secret once. A terse smile appeared on his lips at the irony of the question.

'I think you do. I'm Haasil Sinha. And you?'

She told him her name. Haasil had a deep frown on his face. *This has to be unreal,* he thought.

BOOK I: The Players in Love

Pallavi

The music. The ambience. The vibe. They were all arresting. But when his eyes found her sitting alone on a high stool at the bar, he concluded everyone else around looked cheap compared to her. She was the kind, he thought, gazing at her, who were designed by God as decoys to life's vagaries. For one sight of girls like her and men like him turned amnesiac to their everyday problems. As she looked around the bar casually, he felt an instant contraction of his ball sack, imagining her noticing him. She didn't.

Truth be told, he never thought someone like him could score with her. Not that he was a novice. Being in the dating scene actively for the last three years and hooking up with all possible variations of women, from juicy virgins to tempting MILFs, he was on top of his game. But this one seemed out of his league. And yet the thrill of it made him approach her after watching her for some time. He wanted to find out if she was with anyone. She wasn't. When he reached her, she took him by surprise by initiating the talk.

'Let me warn you, boy,' she said, turning to him the moment he approached her. 'I'm a bloodsucking, ball-busting shapeshifter.' In the hues of the psychedelic light, her canines glistened, and she took a sip of her Absolut. *Damn, she could be right*, he thought.

'I would have been disappointed if you were anything less.' He tried to be his charming best. She looked piercingly into his eyes. Then gave a terse smile. As if in that trice she concluded what she was going to do to him. With him.

The next one hour went by with the two sipping drinks and him doing most of the talking. He noticed she was talking only in monosyllables. It normally meant that the girl was already somewhere else in her mind. *Is she where I want to take her?* he wondered.

'Are you even here?' he asked with amusement on his face to negate any possibility of her taking offence.

'No. I'm upstairs in the hotel. In my room. Getting eaten by you.'

The intensity and seductiveness with which the words escaped her, he somehow managed not to cum then and there.

'Why the delay then?' His heart was racing. Never before had he hunted with so much anticipation. Or was he being hunted here?

'I guess you like to talk.' There was a hint of mockery in the way she said it. He noted it. Asked the bartender to bill the drinks to his room.

'I have a room here,' he said.

'Let's fill the room then,' she said and held his hand. The touch made his heart throb. She pulled him out of the bar amidst strangers drinking and dancing.

In the next three minutes, he had swiped his room's card on the door. He couldn't put the 'Do Not Disturb' sign on the door for she had pushed him to the wall by then, her hands sizing up his tool. He'd never felt a girl grab his groin that hard before. His whisky-scented mouth was licked by her vodka-laced tongue. Their warm breath was urgently diffusing into each other's. She broke the smooch, held his tee in a threatening way as if she was going to punch him. Instead, she pulled him and pushed him on the couch. Her strength surprised him. And aroused him further as well. Ensconced on the couch, he saw her turning her head around.

She noticed a couple of oranges on the centre table. They were complimentary gifts from the hotel. She stretched and grabbed one of them. She held it with one hand and unbuckled him with the other while her mouth started exploring the insides of his cheeks. She grabbed his throbbing, erect penis, and gave the orange to him.

'Peel it,' she demanded. He did as asked. The sudden pause in their carnal journey turned into an ache. The moment he peeled the orange, she snatched it from him and squeezed it hard. The juice trickled on to his penis.

'I like it tangy,' she winked and went down on him. He grabbed her lustrous hair as she deep-throated him. His head reclined, jaws wide open, eyes rolled upwards as if he was ready to breathe out the orgasm he could already feel building inside. Suddenly, he felt her canines on his balls.

'Fuck!' he grunted. Looked down at her. She had her eyes on him. He smirked.

'Does that give you a kick?' he asked, breathing heavily now. She shook her head in the negative.

'My kick lies elsewhere,' she said. He shrugged.

With a swift movement of her hand, she picked up the fruit knife from the table.

'Uncertainty is a kick,' she said and slashed her wrist. Blood started spilling out. The boy's sexual spell vanished in a trice.

'What do you think, will I live or die tonight?' Pallavi said with such a disturbing chuckle that he wondered if she had been serious when she'd said she was a bloodsucking, ball-busting shapeshifter.

Maybe she was worse, he thought. Just that he didn't know. Pallavi collapsed by his side with her bloody hand on his privates.

Haasil

Singapore was supposed to give him some solace. But Haasil Sinha had quickly understood that finding solace by shifting places wasn't possible if the chaos one was running away from was right there in the middle of one's heart.

From the time he had shifted his base to Singapore, Haasil constantly felt a tug-of-war of intense rushes within him. The rush of the past. Of the once-lived true love. And the rush of severing himself from that past. The goddamn accident that altered it all for him.

A part of him desperately wanted to teleport himself to his past and live it like he was living it back then. Smooth, unperturbed, carefree. It wasn't that past which had Pallavi in it, though. It was the one he'd once lived with Palki but, thanks to the accident, now remembered vaguely. And the more he fought this tug-of-war within, the more he felt clawed by the present.

Another part of him was willing to leave it all behind and start anew. But with what? He had no friends in Singapore.

He only had people he knew from work. People who surrounded him in the office, met him over business brunches or accompanied him on weekend work trips. When he was alone in his pad, Haasil felt borderline suicidal. Till then, he had only equated loneliness with 'me time', but there was another kind of loneliness, he understood, being in Singapore, which made one feel worthless. Alienated the person from the world around. And blurred all the sense of life's direction. It made one believe that even if one lived for 10,000 more days, or years, it would all be the same. One was destined to breathe and live a daily staleness of a kind. This feeling was destroying him from within. More so after realizing the hope that Pallavi gave him while feigning to be Palki was a bluff. That Palki was, in all probability, dead by now. There was not a single night when Haasil, before dozing off, had not asked himself: Can a person's present be totally bereft of the past? And never did he go to sleep with any satisfactory answer.

Singapore, as a city, was too concrete for him. Whenever he looked out from his sixty-third-floor balcony, all he could see was aspiration, competition and a disturbing restlessness in the form of skyscrapers, flyovers and buzzing automobiles. A few years ago, all this used to give him a kick. Life was for him to discover. Not any more. His soul sought some solace. Something to hold on to, with which he could ride the waves of life. Or perhaps it had to be *someone*.

Haasil did match with a few women in the beginning, on dating apps. He thought companionship perhaps would help him kill the loneliness. But as he kept meeting women, he understood that companionship couldn't be forced. You could fuck someone one night or more, but you couldn't become someone's soulmate just like that. For that, one needed some basic affinity. And serendipity. He found neither. Eventually, he deleted the dating apps.

Though NH Consultants, the firm that he ran along with his best friend Nitin Punjabi, was going steady, their personal relationship remained strained. Haasil wasn't able to fathom how Nitin could simply substitute his wife Palki with someone else. Just because they looked similar? Just because he was Pallavi's first love? *Bullshit!* If the truth had not come out—that the woman was an imposter—Haasil would have lived a lie all his life. Haasil had accepted Palki's supposed death, but he couldn't justify what Nitin chose to do to his life.

Haasil hadn't shifted to Singapore absolutely alone, though. He had brought with him everything tangible that had belonged to Palki. Her clothes, her cosmetics, her photographs, their wedding albums, their wedding DVD, her jewellery. Everything that he could touch and feel that belonged to Palki. He put them in his apartment in Singapore. Haasil's lonely hours were about looking at, caressing, kissing those things. But instead of happiness, as he thought those things would give him, they underlined the sense of loss within him. Loss is a tricky thing. And it works in phases. The first phase draws you in, severing you from your own present. The next phase comforts you. That's when it turns truly dangerous because it makes one find one's home in it. Haasil realized this one night when he was asked out for dinner by a lady. He was totally free but he cancelled the dinner, citing an important business call. All he did that night was light a candle in front of Palki's photograph and keep crying till the candle burnt out.

Sitting in a salon one day, while his hair was being cut, Haasil had an epiphany when his stylist asked, 'Should I cut these off, sir?'

'These' were a few strands of white hair. Haasil was in his mid-thirties. But not the first one to have white hair at that age thanks to the new-age work and lifestyle stress.

Haasil nodded to his stylist. The strands were cut. The sight of them immersed him in deeper thought.

What was he doing with his life? Today it was a few strands of white hair; soon they would multiply and maybe all of them one day would simply fall off. Then what? Die after living a lonely two or three decades? Palki wasn't going to come back. If she had to, she would have by now. The police were right. She died in the accident itself which he, unfortunately, had survived. And now his life was slowly ending . . . one day at a time. Should he live with the illusion that Palki's belongings were equal to Palki's presence? There's always a lurking fear in the shadows between illusion and reality. And it's that fear which makes people opt for the illusion. Should he break free from the illusion, embrace the fear and look reality in the eye? Should he stop using his pain as a comfort-cushion and make something of the life that was left? Should he stop being a crybaby? And perhaps move on? Perhaps fall in love again. Perhaps live again. Maybe not the way he used to with Palki. But at least *live*.

Haasil Sinha walked out of that salon a changed man. A man who knew how therapeutic self-acceptance could be. How important it was to burst his illusion-balloons that he had inflated with the air of false hope. And that he wasn't doing anything wrong by Palki, or her love for him, by moving on in life. Most pertinent was his realization that when you move on in life, it doesn't necessarily mean you are moving on from the person you promised to traverse this life alongside. By moving on you are simply being more accommodating.

The first thing Haasil did was call up the woman who had asked him out for a drink numerous times. He had rejected her requests every time till then. Sometimes verbally, sometimes textually.

Two nights later, when Haasil had that long overdue drink with her, he didn't know his life was about to change further. For better or for worse were just perspectives. But a change was around the corner for sure. The woman was a co-worker till then. After the drink that night, she became his only friend. Then a series of after-work drinks followed for months, which turned her into his only confidante. Then, six months later, he proposed to her.

She couldn't stop her tears seeing the man of her dreams kneeling down for her, with a ring in his hand and her name on his lips, *Swadha Kashyap, will you marry me?*

Even dreams weren't that dreamy for her.

Swadha

The journey to Singapore had started with hope for her. When Haasil had come to her place, requesting her to join him in managing his Singapore office, it felt as though life was pinching her butt after playing a practical joke on her. It was too good to be true.

After Pallavi had sent her the threatening note telling her to forget Haasil or lose her job, Swadha was more hurt than scared. She wasn't even a threat to their love story. In the nights that followed, what injured her more was the thought that she would lose Haasil forever for no fault of hers. Not that she had ever had him. Professionally, she used to hang around him, be it during boardroom meets or team lunches but personally, she was non-existent for him. And somehow she had accepted that the office was the closest she could ever be with Haasil. She had rejected many lucrative job offers only to be around him. Only to see and sometimes talk to him in the nine or ten hours of office every day. 'I don't want to be your hobby, I want to be your habit,' she had once lamented.

But that was not to be. At least at that point in time when she had read the note.

With the note from Pallavi, Swadha couldn't even be his hobby. After resigning from NH Consultants, Swadha was absolutely blank about her future. More her personal future than her professional one. She had decided to take a break from work, travel, learn a new skill and then get back to life. A day before she was ready to depart for her sabbatical, a solo Europe trip, was when she saw Haasil at her doorstep requesting her to resume her role at NH Consultants. The butterflies in her stomach, though, only started to flap when she sat in the business class seat beside him, flying to Singapore for real.

The news of Palki's supposed death and Pallavi's substitution of her did upset Swadha. Because it upset Haasil. It was during the flight that they started talking. Not like professionals. The monosyllabic replies told her he was emotionally loaded. The constant shaking of his legs, the running of his fingers through his hair, told her there was some restlessness within him. After pondering about it for some time, Swadha put a nervous hand on his, trying her best to make it look like a friendly gesture and said, 'I'm a good listener. Try me if you ever want to.' There was a momentary eye lock. Swadha felt something had melted within her. There's nothing more emotionally arousing than the person you love looking deep into your eyes and making you believe there could be a thirsty soul within waiting for you, Swadha thought. What happened in the immediate moment following was something she had not expected.

The man whom she had desired so intensely since she lay her eyes on him had his head on her shoulder. He cried profusely with a constant shiver. Swadha didn't know what her reaction should be. A little patting of his back? Or caressing it? Telling him everything will be all right? She did none of those. Instead, she sat still, feeling the grasp of their hands tighten with every passing second. Once Haasil was done, he looked up at her, warm tears running down his cheeks.

'Thanks for not interrupting,' he said, then excused himself to go to the washroom. Swadha sat there motionless. Caressing her own palm with her fingers to feel his touch. For the first time, her skin felt different to her. It had his dry tears. She felt that he, unknowingly, had given something intimate of himself to her. Something a man gives only to select women in his life. Something that did not define him as the man he is but actually *makes* him the man he is. With that feeling reaching a realization, something matured inside her. She wasn't the *silly Jilly* any more.

Living in Singapore, Swadha too was alone. She had a group of three college friends working in Singapore. All married. They used to be her weekend getaway. Though she didn't tell any of them about Haasil. Being the only single person in the group, her friends did try to get her hooked up, but Swadha turned them down politely every time. In her mind, she was dating Haasil since she had joined NH Consultants. This time, though, she was more proactive.

Swadha made sure she asked Haasil out even when the slightest chance beckoned. At times, she even let her self-respect take a back seat and approached him without waiting for him to take the lead. But Haasil rarely met her after work hours. And when he did, it was with four other people from their office core team. Every 'no' from him was like a punch to her heart. There were times when she felt that Haasil wasn't ignorant about her feelings. Those moments were all the more difficult. Did he ask me to rejoin only because he liked my work? Nothing about me? In a short span, she had had three different hairstyles. She started taking extra care of herself. Numerous skin and hair treatments, contact lenses replaced her spectacles and wedges were replaced with high heels. When nothing worked, one night, sloshed at one of her friends' house parties, she realized that perhaps Haasil wasn't comfortable with her any more after showcasing his weak side to her on the flight to Singapore.

It was only when she visited his pad for a work meet with other colleagues that she chanced upon the room which was set up as Palki's room. As if she lived there. It was scary. Swadha realized the problem was deeper and more personal than she had assumed. And it didn't involve her. She understood he needed healing, not necessarily love. Or maybe healing that comes with love alone. She knew she could give him all the love, but would she be able to heal him? If not a soulmate, could she be his healmate? That was something Haasil had to decide.

After seeing Palki's room in his pad, Swadha gave up asking him out for coffee, dinner or brunches. Her heart ached. But every time he liked one of her posts on Instagram, she could never stop blushing either. Till one day that one thing happened which she was hoping for but never expected. Haasil asked her out for drinks after work. She excused herself to go to the office washroom, cried like a baby, then came back and went out with him.

One dine-n-drinks led to many more. With every dinner, endless conversations happened. With these, she inched closer to him. An unprecedented ease had come up between them. While in the office, she received the same professional vibe she was used to before; the after-work vibe changed. Swadha felt the intimacy ascending every time he dropped her below her apartment after their long, verbose after-work dinners. The dichotomy aroused her but confused her as well. The arousal remained and the confusion was erased when, dropping her home one night, Haasil gave her a peck on her cheek. He drove off the next second. She stood there for a good five minutes, unable to move. Her heart was racing. Her mind was blank. The hair on the nape of her neck had risen. And she was wet between her thighs. She didn't need a mirror to tell her who was the most beautiful person in this world at that moment. She went up to her place beaming.

The next week, during one of their casual dine-outs, Haasil proposed to her. She felt so emotionally choked that she couldn't speak for some time. Haasil thought it was a no. Her tears along with her smile convinced him otherwise.

Swadha informed her family in Lucknow. Within the immediate fortnight, Haasil and Swadha flew back to India. Haasil, at her behest, did inform Nitin and his fiancée Sanjana about the engagement and the legal marriage. The two childhood friends did hug it out emotionally before the ceremony.

Haasil didn't want a lavish wedding. The couple decided to make the ring ceremony their only party thrown for friends and family. The ring exchange was followed by a signing of the legal nuptial papers. Swadha officially became Mrs Swadha Kashyap Sinha. There was no time to think or blink. The spontaneity with which everything happened made it seem like a fairy tale to her. Two days later, they flew to the Maldives for their honeymoon.

Sitting close together in the seaplane, looking at the picturesque island below and then at a curious Haasil clicking pictures of it like a kid, she prayed that their love story remained insulated from all kinds of evil eyes. This was something she couldn't afford to lose. Come. What. May.

Palki

There will always be that one twilight zone within the logical understanding of mankind where the happening of certain things will forever remain unexplained. Perhaps it's pure chance, as purists would term it, but there's a whole school of people who, when they witness such unbelievable events, simply look up at the sky and claim, 'God wanted it this way.' Palki's survival story fell into that category.

Hariharan's guruji's prophecy turned out to be true even though there was no science connected to it. As predicted by him, after serving Palki for a year and miraculously getting her back on her feet again with only indigenous herbs, Hariharan's wife had become pregnant. Nine months later, she delivered twin sons. Luva and Kusha, they named them. Hariharan was overjoyed. He went to the same guruji to offer his oblation. After him, the next oblation to be given was to the goddess, or so Hariharan and his wife believed, who had visited their home for a year and blessed them with enough good luck in the form of renewed fertility to bear children after fifteen years of their marriage.

Hariharan himself had prepared payasam. After presenting the local sweet to his babu, under whom he used to work in the state forest near Bengaluru, a happy Hariharan headed home to touch the woman's feet whose presence had turned their wheel of fortune. But once home, he couldn't find her there. Or anywhere. He asked his wife, who was busy with the babies.

'She was here only.' The wife sounded as bewildered as Hariharan, for never before had the woman left their hut without them knowing it. She used to talk a little and in languages that they knew were Hindi and English but didn't understand one bit. For the next half hour, Hariharan looked for the woman everywhere in his village but couldn't locate her. He couldn't ask anyone about her because he had told nobody since he had found her all bruised and injured from the accident site. That was another of his guruji's rules. *You can't talk about her to anyone except me.* When he came back to his hut, clueless about the woman's whereabouts, his wife was ready with an answer.

'I think she indeed was a goddess. She was here till we had our babies. And now she is gone. Disappeared.' She had a profound glimmer in her eyes as if she was still reeling from the woman's residual aura in the hut. Hearing his wife, a hint of belief twinkled in Hariharan's eyes. It reminded him of one of his guruji's teachings that we all have certain roles to play not only in our life but in others' lives as well. And once that role is fulfilled, the meaning of the person's presence blurs. Hariharan sighed, realizing he didn't need to seek the woman any more. He sat down beside his wife and admired the two little bundles of joy in their life.

Fifteen kilometres away from the hut, Palki had settled herself in a private bus that used to take people living in and around the forest to the city for all kinds of labour-related work.

Looking out of the bus window, she wondered why she couldn't remember anything about her previous life any more. Was it possible to forget oneself totally? She had seen Hariharan and his wife taking utmost care of her from the time she could barely open her eyes to the time when she could walk on her own. Initially, a majority of her time went by in sleeping. When she started having some prolonged conscious sense, Palki realized she had innumerable bruises and injuries. It was Hariharan's wife who used to apply some paste on her wounds and bathe her for the longest time. Palki guessed the paste must have been medicinal in nature.

But Palki couldn't bring herself to develop any emotional attachment with them. Majorly because she understood early that verbal communication wasn't possible with them. It made her impatient within. She did try to escape the hut a few times but wasn't able to, since one of the two always remained homebound, keeping an eye on her. For a long time, Palki didn't see any other human being except for Hariharan and his wife.

One month before she escaped the hut, Palki had started to help Hariharan's wife with some household chores. That was only because the wife was heavily pregnant. Palki had thought that the day she delivered, she would leave them. Where to? She didn't know. She would simply follow her instinct. Seeing Hariharan going out while the wife was busy with the babies, Palki walked out wearing the wife's clothes.

Palki walked on, non-stop, till she reached the highway where she noticed a bus parked by the side. She saw people queuing up to get on it. Males, females, kids. Palki went and stood at the end of the line. Though the handyman had his doubts looking at her, it was clear to him she wasn't a local.

He tried to communicate with her but Palki's silence made him assume she was deaf and dumb. He didn't bother her further. He made sure she got a seat by the window.

As the wind hit her face, Palki tried her best for the umpteenth time to remember who she was, where she belonged to, who had been with her, her family, her identity, her name . . . but nothing came to her. Except tears in her eyes. She had turned into a ghost with no memories, no past. And for someone like Palki, the problem with no semblance of any past was she didn't know where to begin her present from.

The bus slowed down after thirteen hours. As Palki looked out of the window, she saw an under-construction site. As the bus entered its main gate, she noticed a huge board on it which read: JPG College of Engineering. The words made sense to her. She could not only read them but understood what they stood for. As the bus halted, Palki could see heaps of sacks, mortar and bricks all around.

As others started stepping down from the bus, Palki looked anxious. She wondered if she had committed a mistake by leaving Hariharan's hut just like that. The world suddenly seemed to be a huge ocean and she was the lone fish who had to create her own survival amidst whales and sharks. Palki started feeling a knot tighten in her stomach. It happened whenever she felt scared. And every time she felt so, a name appeared on her lips. A name that she had muttered many times before. *Haasil*. A name that was tattooed on her hips as well. Along with another name.

Palki-Haasil, the tattoo read. Neither made any sense to her.

If only Palki knew those two names locked a life that she had no memory of but, once upon a time, she used to swear by.

Pallavi

The boy who took Pallavi to the hotel room and found his confidence punctured when he saw her slash her own wrist, panicked as if it was he who was going to die. When Pallavi didn't respond after he soft-slapped her cheeks, he could feel his balls curl up. *Fuck, is she dead?* He picked up his clothes and scampered out of the room, half naked. He had dressed up by the time he reached the floor elevator. Then he went to the reception to report what had happened in the room. Excluding the sex part. Though the room was booked in his name, he didn't go in till he noticed, while sitting in the lobby and chewing his nails, Pallavi being taken out on a stretcher by some hospital staff.

Pallavi was rushed to the emergency section of a nearby hospital. The junior doctors went into action. And in the next half an hour, they realized Pallavi was brought in just in the nick of time, so she hadn't lost a fatal amount of blood. She came back to her senses seven hours later. And the first thought she had after realizing she was in a hospital room was that the junior doctor treating her was cute.

From the moment Pallavi had torn up the letter she had written to Haasil years back, justifying her actions, her intentions and her love for him, she had turned into an intricate chaos. A directionless storm. A woman on the edge. Though she had returned home asking her mother to find a match for her, deep within she had lost her mojo in life. She preferred to remain constantly high, constantly disconnected from life. Alcohol became her water. She had no idea what her tomorrow would be like. Pallavi was all instinct, zero plans. But she started taking the spontaneity to a dangerous level when one day, a year after Haasil had thrown her out of his life, she slashed herself sitting in a hotel room. And then went dancing. She wanted to see if she was destined to live or not. It was her way of mocking life. For it had mocked her enough using one name. One man. *Dino* . . . *Haasil*. Her one true and first love.

When Pallavi had come home from Haasil's place to ask her mother to arrange for her marriage, Mrs Vimani thought she was dreaming. She double-checked it with her. And both times Pallavi was affirmative. She wanted to settle down. Or so she told them. Mr and Mrs Vimani felt a burden had been lifted from their ageing shoulders. They assumed their foster-daughter had had enough of her wild life. Perhaps her traditional woman's instinct of becoming someone's wife and a mother had been triggered. Perhaps she was ready to coalesce with societal norms. But when they saw the bandage on her wrist, they understood Pallavi had become a complicated ball of chaos.

In the week that Pallavi came back from the hospital, Mr and Mrs Vimani set up a meeting with one of the prospective grooms, a Gujarati NRI boy who had just taken over from his father's automobile business in London. A brunch was arranged in New Delhi's Taj hotel by Mr Vimani. All through the brunch, there was a gleam in the boy's eyes seeing Pallavi. As if he would be happiest if she were married to him. And that ticked her off. How could she be a reason for a man's happiness? She felt an instant hatred for him. It was as visceral an emotion as was her heartbreak decades ago. Or the heartache when the only one—Haasil Sinha—to whom she had surrendered in life refused to acknowledge her perspective. Instead of appreciating her will to heal him, Haasil had labelled her an imposter. A part of it was true. She was not Palki. But what about her love for him? What about her intentions for him? Those weren't imposters.

Pallavi not only walked out of the brunch, but also her home. Once and for all. *Whom was she kidding anyway?* Domestic life wasn't for her. But did she deserve the scar given to her as a teenager? Who decides who gets scarred and who doesn't? There was no answer. Life coaches would say it's all about how you handle your experience. *Horsefuckingshit!* There was actually no answer. And because there was no answer, it infuriated Pallavi even further. Noticing the gleam in the Gujarati NRI boy's eyes, she finally understood what her purpose was in this world. To scar men. As much as possible. As many as possible. And in between, when she felt like mocking life, Pallavi took a bet on her destiny by trying to kill herself. The more she lived, the more she believed her destiny was to screw men up.

Pallavi settled into a flat in Gurugram, sharing it with a friend till she joined a premier airline. Seeing her work experience, she was made the cabin crew head. After a few months, she shifted into a studio apartment alone. And from then on, all hell broke loose on the men whom she swiped right on Tinder, Bumble and later Hinge. Her pictures were genuine there, but her name and details were not. It was part of the plan to execute her purpose.

The latest one, however, didn't even need her to swipe right. Dr Mayank Gupta was the junior doctor treating her since she was brought from the hotel as an emergency case. Before she had been discharged, Pallavi had kept a phone number for him on the notepad in the room she was admitted in. That very evening, he called her up. They decided to meet for a drink but by then Pallavi had blocked him from her real profile on all her social media. Later in the evening, when she met Mayank, Pallavi told him she wasn't into social media as it affected her mental health. And fed him complete lies about herself. A month later, they planned a trip to Himachal Pradesh on his bike.

'It's weird, but it feels like I never lived without you,' Pallavi said, cuddling into his arm. Mayank was the seventeenth guy she had been with that year.

'I swear, I feel the same,' he said.

Trekking in Himachal, they had set up a tent close to Triund. There was nobody around except for the sound of a drizzle and wind. The lovemaking, or that's how Mayank termed it, lasted for a good half hour. Pallavi was demanding while Mayank, to safeguard his masculinity in front of her, didn't complain even though he was exhausted within the first fifteen minutes itself. He had never seen or met a woman like her. The areas she reached in him, no woman ever had. One second she was yelling in his ear that she was coming, the other second she was demanding a change of position. Unpredictability had a new face for him. By now, one thing he was sure of, she was the one for him. His soulmate.

Mayank had been with many girls in the past but nobody made him feel in love so intensely, so insanely. Back then, he had always wondered what the feeling would be like to be crazily in love with someone. Like when someone casts a spell over you. Like you see nothing beyond the person, like you want nothing except the person. Now he knew. In his mind, Mayank had promised himself he would take her to meet his family once they returned from the trek. Girls like her shouldn't be allowed much time. You get them, you be with them forever, he concluded.

While knitting sweet dreams of their collective future, Mayank dozed off with a wide, stupid, orgasmic smile on his face. Once Pallavi was sure he was asleep, she took a deep breath, feeling accomplished. Another male would be scarred soon. And that would give the green-eyed monster within the happiness she was seeking in the name of purpose-in-life.

Pallavi dressed up, blocked his number on her phone, collected her stuff and then vanished from the place. And his life. At most he would use the address on her Aadhaar card that she had used during her hospital stay and it would lead him to her parents who themselves didn't know where exactly their daughter was.

She knew she had left Mayank, like sixteen more guys before, thirsty with questions. Just as life had once done to her. Why didn't Haasil choose her? Why didn't *he* understand her love for him? Why didn't *he* apologize to her for his rudeness? For questioning her intent? Her love for him? Why didn't *Haasil* . . . that sonofabitch . . . whose tattoo she was carrying not on her skin—but on her soul. Like an open wound which could catch infection any time. En route to New Delhi, she was already swiping right on the dating apps.

Haasil–Swadha

They stayed in the Maldives for a week. A week every night of which Swadha used to look up at the star-studded sky, then at Haasil, pinch herself and giggle intoxicatedly with new-found happiness. It was a dream that she never thought was possible in this very life. She was both alert and numb at the same time. If someone shook her and told her this was a dream, she would have believed the person. She couldn't possibly be married to Haasil Sinha. *No way!* She couldn't possibly be honeymooning with him. *Pinch me, someone!*

Haasil had booked the Muraka for their first night there. Swadha couldn't hold back her excitement when she realized it was an underwater hotel. She was awed by it after recently seeing it on an actor's Instagram, who had spent her honeymoon there. Her jaw dropped at the prospect of sleeping underwater with the love of her life right beside her.

After they checked in and were ushered to their suite, Swadha spent ten minutes admiring the different corners of the suite and clicking pictures. Exotic fish were constantly swimming about and hitting the glass dome above, which was the suite's ceiling. The entire suite looked magical. Haasil could feel the happiness emanating from her. She hugged him tight, finishing her short recce.

'You happy?' he asked. Swadha found herself too choked to even utter one word. She simply nodded, wiped the tears from her eyes and gave Haasil a hard peck. When she went to the washroom and got ready for a quick shower, it struck her that they would be intimate for the first time. Their dating phase had been pretty short and all they did was smooch. And a little touching here and there. Haasil didn't initiate anything more, nor did she. Perhaps the thought that the man of her dreams was going to marry her was enough for her to rejoice. Even the wedding happened in such a fast-forward manner that they found their tired selves sleeping instantly on their proverbial first nuptial night.

Now, looking at her naked self in the mirror, Swadha hoped he liked what she had to offer. All said, lust played a role in laying the foundation of love in a marriage. Or so she had read somewhere. Swadha was a virgin. So much so that she had not even kissed any man till now except Haasil. For one half of her life she had remained single because she hadn't got anyone interested in her, the other half she was single because she only loved and desired Haasil. As a virgin, she had a lot on her 'to do' list. One of them she did right before her wedding. She underwent the painful Brazilian wax. Seeing herself naked, she felt sexual as never before. It made her nervous for she didn't want to disappoint Haasil in any way. For the first time a man, her husband, would see her stark naked.

After having caviar, oysters and steaks for dinner over some expensive champagne, Swadha and Haasil were back in their suite. They were laughing at some joke when both stopped together. There was a sudden, haunting silence. The reflection of the light through the clean water above cascaded on them through the thick glass wall, making them look surreal for the other.

Haasil came up to her. The proximity wasn't awkward. But the intimacy it brought was. In a good way. She felt his kiss on her lips. She felt her heart throbbing while she turned warm. As she reciprocated his kiss, closing her eyes, she felt nothing mattered then. The past, the present, the future were mere existential excuses. Haasil held the tip of her zipper on the back of her black dress and slid it down. The sound of it tearing the silence further aroused her. Swadha's back was open. She felt goosebumps appear on her skin. Keeping her eyes closed, she helped Haasil get rid of his tee. The next to hit the floor were his trousers. As she felt urgent kisses on her face, she helped him take off her dress completely. And when she opened her eyes now, she felt she was living a fantasy of hers. Everything was perfect. Caressing Haasil's chest, which was shapely with sparse hair, she felt wet like never before. They smooched with Haasil guiding her hand over his underwear. She felt his hard penis. Her first thought was whether it would fit inside her. She broke the smooch and looked at Haasil. He shot back an expectant look.

'I'm a virgin. I thought you should know before . . .' Swadha's voice had a hint of apology. Haasil found it cute. He smiled at her, lifted her up and a few steps later, they were on the bed. Seconds later, they were stark naked. Swadha's first instinct was to cover herself up with the blanket but Haasil didn't let her. She was thankful for that. He kissed her all over. And using his tongue, drew an H on her navel.

Was it his way of marking her? That was the last she could think straight as by then, Haasil's tongue had reached her waxed vagina. He was gentle to begin with but switched gears in between. Swadha chose to simply react to Haasil's actions.

What followed for the next two to three hours was more like a lucid dream. Its aftertaste remained a vague feeling once Haasil lay beside her, fully spent. They hadn't used any protection. She intentionally didn't go to wash herself. As Swadha felt him take her into a bear hug, with him sleeping almost immediately, she noticed, beyond the orgasmic glow, there was a semblance of peace on his face. *Peace after having her?* Swadha felt blessed as she hugged him tight.

Flashes of her first interview in front of him, years ago, occurred to her. Her mind was sifting through all the moments which led to this one. The interview, her unintentional blunders, the elevator incident, the dropping her home, flying to Singapore . . . in hindsight, Swadha realized there were quite a few moments they had spent together before arriving in Singapore. *Destiny works in crazy ways*, Swadha thought, closing her eyes.

The next day they shifted to an ocean villa at another resort. Though they had pre-planned their activities for the day, they cancelled everything, making love all day, cuddling up in the hammock outside their villa at night. Their tired, naked bodies were wrapped in one single blanket as they saw the dawn breaking, with the sun peeping out a bit on the horizon. Hands tightly clasped, they didn't speak much. Both were lost in their own thoughts, but every now and then they did inadvertently start smooching till their jaws ached. Then they were immersed in silence again.

It was during breakfast that they started talking. Swadha had the most to say. She filled him up on all the stupid things she used to think about, seeing him in office. Haasil had an inkling about her feelings, but only when she confessed things in detail did he realize how hopelessly Swadha was in love with him.

In their ocean villa, they preferred to listen to their favourite music as they bundled up in the hammock, naked, looking at the expanse of the ocean in front. When they had emptied two bottles of wine, cuddled up, she thought of asking him a question that had been with her since the time she had said yes to his proposal.

'Do you miss her?'

Haasil understood who she was talking about. Certainly not Pallavi.

He glanced at her once and then at the vast expanse which joined on to a beatific dark horizon. He took time to dress his feelings with words.

'I do, yeah. Probably, I always will.'

A few minutes of silence later, Haasil said, 'I hope you didn't mind that. If you did, I apologize.'

'It's all right. I appreciate the fact that you didn't say no to please me. Honesty is important between people who are trying to live a life together.'

'Indeed,' Haasil said. *But how honest can the honesty be is the question*, he thought.

The kind of intimacy and warmth Swadha felt being with Haasil was unprecedented for her. She'd never been this close to any male. It made his constant care for her all the more alluring. His concern all the more soul-pleasing. And his latent protectiveness all the more arousing. *If this was what man–woman dynamics was all about*, she thought, *I now get it why people so desperately want the right person in their life.*

There was respect in his eyes when he talked to her. 'Are you okay?', 'Are you comfortable?' were his first questions whenever they went out together. The following five days of their honeymoon went in a haze. They went kayaking, scuba-diving and did some adrenaline-pumping water sports, but all she remembered was Haasil's smiling face during those experiences. He looked happy with her. And that gave her more intense emotional orgasms than the ones he led her to, being inside her on the bed.

On the last night at the resort, after dinner, they decided to take a walk by the beach under the moonlight. There was a slight chill in the air as Swadha and Haasil traipsed hand in hand.

'I confessed everything but did you ever see me like . . .' Swadha didn't know how to complete what she had in mind without sounding childish.

'. . . how you would be naked?' Haasil had a sly smile on his face.

'No! I meant you could have imagined that as well, but what I'm trying to ask is whether knowing me has made you happy.'

'Of course, why else would I have proposed?'

Haasil had a point, or so Swadha thought. Then another question popped up in her head.

'Actually, why did you propose to me? I know it must have been so obvious with me asking you out for a drink so many times. Please say no else I'll disappear into thin air right now.' Swadha looked acutely embarrassed.

Haasil laughed before speaking, 'To be honest, it was obvious. But then you don't end up proposing to anyone and everyone who asks you out repeatedly.'

'So what was it about me?' Swadha asked, trying to conceal her blushes.

'That you are uncomplicated. Talking to you, I understood you have a simple way of looking at things. I envied you for that. Sometimes, with that kind of perspective, you spare yourself a lot of mental and emotional shit. And so . . .'

Haasil couldn't complete his sentence. Swadha had pressed her mouth on to his. They smooched standing under the night sky. When they broke apart, Haasil noticed something.

'Look there,' he said. Swadha followed his gaze on to the calm ocean where, at some distance, the moonlight was falling on it, making an ethereal spotlight.

'Let's go,' Haasil said. She saw him doff his tee, shorts and then his underwear as well.

'Skinny-dipping?' She looked amazed. Haasil responded by helping her strip to her skin. He pulled her into the ocean. The water was cold. It took them some seconds to reach the moonlit spotlight. Half drowned in the clean water, feeling the moonlight bathe their exposed skin, they smooched once again. Life seemed as if it had a divine plan for them.

Except Haasil was glad Swadha had smooched him on time. For he was in two minds whether he should tell her why exactly he had proposed to her. 20 per cent of it was because of what he had told her. 80 per cent he hadn't. *And perhaps I never will*, Haasil thought as he tightened his grasp on her back.

Pallavi

Mayank did try hard but he couldn't reach Pallavi. Not that she cared. Pallavi had been staying in Mumbai for a month now because of her flying schedule. Mayank, anyway, was told she was a chef at some resort in Jaisalmer. Setting men on a wild goose chase after ghosting them made her feel at peace with herself.

It was a day off for her. Pallavi was in her room in the Westin, Mumbai. Stretching her legs on the table and looking out from her thirty-second-floor room on to the city's non-stop hustle visible through the huge glass wall. It was a visual echo of her within. No matter how much she kept herself busy, the traffic of her hurt, her injuries, her let-downs was hustling within for her constant attention. When she wasn't busy, it was a bottle of Absolut that kept the inner noise at bay.

Pallavi was already one bottle of Absolut down. She poured some from the second bottle into her glass, grabbed some cubes from the ice bucket, rubbed them on to her forehead for a few seconds and then dropped them into the glass. She gulped down the drink in one go. She could feel boredom developing. Ghosting men alone wasn't working. She needed some new experience, a change of gear because she was used to this. And Pallavi could never bear being used to anything in life.

Pallavi's phone buzzed for the umpteenth time. The sound of the notification was customized. She knew exactly which app's notification it was. Bumble. She had a total of fifty-three matches waiting for her response. Most of them were hot males. Any girl would go weak in the knees imagining a prospective hook-up with them but Pallavi's mind was elsewhere. She was wondering . . .

Let's say I match with one of these hotbod morons. He would say some cheesy, smart-ass lines. I would reply with some more. We both would try to throw our sense of humour at the other. Hey-look-how-smart-I-am kind of a thing. That would make us believe, even if for some time that is, ah, this person seems fun and interesting. We would then exchange numbers or decide to meet at some public place. If we exchange numbers, then a few phone calls and some late-night WhatsApp messages later we would meet. If our hormones are raging, then it will be a pub, else a café. Knowing myself, it will be a pub. We will be at our tempting best look-wise. Some more talk that won't add up to anything in my life. We would drink till reality became elusive, then some intimate dancing would follow. Then we would head straight to either his place or my room here in the hotel. Followed by the obvious. And for the next few weeks, I would make him believe I was the purpose he was waiting for in life. Then I'll ghost him. Never to think about him again. While he would constantly wonder what he had done wrong. And make me a part of his life. He won't ever forget me.

That last bit was a sadistic high for her. The moment the train of thoughts ended, Pallavi realized what had changed for her. For the first time in life, she was ahead of life. She knew its moves. And when you move ahead of the opponent's game, thrill ceases to exist. Her phone rang with a video call alert. Pallavi glanced at who was calling. It was her bestie from the airlines.

'Yeah, Shivi,' Pallavi said.

'OMG, what happened? You never sounded so bored ever!'

'I know. I can feel it in my bones. I think I'll be the first person ever who died of boredom. There's no thrill left in my life. Should I slash myself again to know if I should even live any more?'

'Shut up! You have changed God knows how many boyfriends in this month alone. What more thrill do you want?'

'Umm . . . wait.' Pallavi placed the phone in a way so Shivi could see almost the entire room.

As Shivi waited on the video call, she noticed Pallavi put the mute button on, then saw her calling someone from the room's desk phone. Then she disappeared from the frame for some time. Shivi waited impatiently. When Pallavi was back in the frame, she had only a towel wrapped around her bosom.

'I know you have a sexy bod, babes. But showing me won't help much,' Shivi quipped. She heard the room's doorbell ring. And looked hard into her phone as Pallavi adjusted her phone's camera view so the room's door came into the frame now. Pallavi went ahead to the door, opened it and then, while taking in a couple of mineral water bottles, intentionally dropped her towel. Shivi's jaw dropped with a loud 'haaw' that came through the phone's speaker. The hotel staff guy rushed away, slamming the door. Shivi still had her hand on her mouth while Pallavi laughed her ass off. She picked up the towel and came towards the phone.

'That's thrill. To show a stranger your boobies,' Pallavi said, still laughing. 'You should have seen his face. It was like *he* was naked.'

'Pallo, this is too much! We keep coming to this hotel all the time. He may share this with his colleagues.'

'Look at him, look at me. Do you really think anyone's going to believe him if he says that I flashed him?'

'Still, yaar, you're nuts.'

'You won't get it. So dang it.' Pallavi paused to light up a smoke.

'All right, whatever! I'm going to the spa downstairs. Will it be thrilling enough for you to join me there?' Shivi asked.

Half an hour later, both the girls gifted themselves a prolonged spa treatment.

'I always wonder if what they show in porn happens for real. Like there the masseur is always a Johnny Sins prototype,' Shivi said, smacking her lips. Her eyes were closed while her face had a funny, orgasmic expression. The girls massaging them laughed in a hushed way. So did Pallavi, who was lying on the adjacent bed, face down. Both girls had wet towels on their naked bodies covering their privates.

'If it happened for real, they wouldn't have cared to show it. Porn is fantasy served on a platter,' said Pallavi.

Shivi made a face. As if Pallavi had punctured her fantasy bubble instead of expanding it. She remained quiet, revelling in the massage for the next hour. Once Shivi was done, she went for a steam session in the attached room while Pallavi chose to take some extra massage time.

The quietude of the spa was broken by a lady's voice. She was talking loudly on her phone standing in the spa lobby. An irked Pallavi could hear her clearly.

'Can't you ask the bitch to keep it low?' Pallavi asked the masseuse.

'Sorry, ma'am. She is a guest,' came the meek response.

Pallavi was almost done with her massage. With the lady's verbal throw, Pallavi could make out she was a typical one who had grown up with loads of money and zero life experience. Once done, Pallavi peeped out of the room before going for the steam bath. The fact that the woman's hands had mehndi and were loaded with bangles told Pallavi that she must be newly married. A man, of course, never needed anything to announce to the world that he was taken. Except probably a ring, which he could take off at any opportune moment. But a taken woman . . . alas!

Shivi came out of the shower but Pallavi was more interested in the lady's conversation. As she spoke further on the phone, Pallavi could make out she must have been talking to her BFF. But what sounded offensive to her was the way the lady was praising her husband. It seemed as though her parents had ventured on an intergalactic expedition only to be back with the best male specimen in the whole goddamn universe solely for her. Listening to her, Pallavi had already made a mental sketch of the husband in her mind. And when her chat concluded, Pallavi wanted to check if her image matched with the real man. It would be a once-in-a-lifetime chance for her to scar such a limited edition of the male species.

While Shivi went back to her room to sleep, Pallavi took her own sweet time in her shower and then waited outside in the spa lobby so she could move out with the woman. By then she had dug out her name from the spa reception. Mrs Shalini Shah.

She followed Shalini to the swimming pool side of the hotel. As she stood by the pool, Pallavi noticed a man swim up to her. Shalini bent down and kissed him.

How about not destroying a man alone this time . . . but a complete marriage? A complete love story, Pallavi wondered, with a devilish smirk. Seeing Shalini gush over the man, Pallavi felt it in her guts that phase two of her life's purpose had been triggered. She beamed.

If only she knew that what she had seen by the pool was just a half-truth.

Haasil–Swadha

Coming back from their dreamy honeymoon and sinking into work life together was more frustrating than difficult. Swadha wanted the honeymoon to stretch. Truth be told, so did Haasil. But they both knew even if they had the honeymoon for a month, instead of a week, they would have still felt the same. Haasil decided to work harder and go for Honeymoon 2.0 in six months. For Swadha, being close to him on a daily basis was a honeymoon itself.

While discussing a project, sitting in the boardroom with a couple of other colleagues, Swadha glanced at herself in the table's glass reflection. She saw a woman in corporate attire wearing a dash of vermilion in her hair parting. There was no pressure from Haasil to use it. But it was her choice. Every time she noticed it, she felt she belonged to someone. Someone whose reality she'd been forever longing to be a part of. Swadha glanced back at Haasil. She had a hint of a sly smile. Haasil did notice but preferred to continue with the meeting that he was leading. Once it was over, he stopped her while the others went out of the boardroom.

'Why were you giving me those looks?' he asked, sounding amused.

Swadha smiled and said, 'Nothing, nothing.' She was on her way out of the boardroom when Haasil held her hand.

'You have to tell me.'

As Swadha moistened her lips, there was the shadow of an unlikely naughtiness on her face.

'There was a time when I used sit with you during meetings and fantasize about you.'

'Really?' Haasil looked incredulous, trying to lock his eyes with hers.

'Don't do that. I'll feel conscious.' She didn't know where to look.

Haasil scurried to the door and locked it from the inside. He turned towards Swadha.

'May I know what Mr Husband is up to?' Swadha asked with a frown.

'Now tell me, what did you imagine in your fantasy?'

Swadha had a twinkle in her eyes. She understood what Haasil had on his mind. It made her feel funny in her tummy.

'That we are alone in the boardroom. While others are working outside.'

'That's done. Next?'

'That I approach you and strip you bare.'

'Uh-huh. In your imagination you are the . . .'

'Dominant. I know.' Swadha came to Haasil and started stripping him. When his blazer, shirt and vest were on the floor, Swadha unbuckled his belt, unzipped his pants and then, holding them along with the elastic of his underwear, knelt down. His hard-on made her moisten her lips.

Haasil gave her an inquiring look. Swadha took his hard penis into her mouth. Neither spoke for some time. The room was filled with muffled gagging sounds. When Swadha's jaws ached a little, she looked up.

'Was I the only one naked in your fantasy?' Haasil asked.

Swadha smiled and shook her head in the negative. Haasil held her shoulders and made her stand up. His tongue made an urgent entry into her mouth.

Swadha didn't have to narrate her fantasy any more. It happened exactly the way she had imagined it all the time. Swadha noted, this time too, Haasil marked an 'H' on her back with his tongue while stripping her. As he took her right on the boardroom table, she found it difficult to keep her moans in check, feeling his tongue explore the wetness between her legs. By now, Haasil knew even the slightest touch on her inner thighs made for a prolonged tickle. He exploited that knowledge to his heart's content. The thrusts, when they happened, were harder than they were during their honeymoon. Probably, the forbidden nature of the act in the office made Haasil do so, Swadha thought. She had to close her mouth tight else she knew she would have screamed her lungs out. By the end of it, Swadha felt she wouldn't get her breath back. Haasil, in particular, was way more intense and lasted longer than usual.

Once done, both quickly dressed up. There was a knock on the door. Haasil hastily opened it. It was his PA.

'Sir, the next meeting needs to happen now. They've been waiting long. Should I make them sit inside?' she asked and then noticed the bin beside the door. It was full of tissues. She glanced at Swadha who had by then managed to put on her dress and was busy getting into her footwear. Her make-up was almost gone.

'I'll ask them to wait a little more,' the PA answered herself and rushed out, closing the door.

'You think she guessed it?' Swadha sounded scandalized.

'It's my office, you are my wife. I'm not accountable to anyone,' Haasil quipped. And left. Swadha's post-coitus glow intensified on hearing it.

Though the honeymoon was over, the dream continued. They could have eaten from the office caterer but Swadha made sure she packed *dabbas* from home. She intentionally used to eat slowly. Watching Haasil eat what she had prepared gave her a high. It used to be her golden hour. No talk. Only smiles as they had their meal together. And every time she felt she was living something that was too good to be real, Swadha used to pinch herself hard, telling herself that she wished to live in this loop forever.

One day, when Swadha felt her chums' cramps, she decided to take the day off. Haasil promised her he'd be back home before his normal time. During lunchtime, she moved out of their master bedroom and was heading towards the kitchen when she stopped by the other room. It was the third bedroom in the pad. She always wanted to ask Haasil why the room's door was kept closed but never got the time to do so. Neither did he tell her ever, except for saying that he had kept a few of Palki's things there before their wedding. Swadha already knew that much when she had been there earlier. But after the wedding, Haasil said he had done away with them. Then why lock an empty room? Swadha never got an answer. Standing by the door, she wondered if she should peep into the room once. She did check the room the day she had shifted. It had a couple of locked wardrobes in it, which Haasil had told her had nothing important. Filled with the excitement of sharing a home with Haasil, she had had other things to think about back then.

Swadha went ahead, held the room's doorknob and rotated it. As she opened the door, she noticed the room looked the same as it did when she had seen it for the first time. There was nothing in it except the wardrobes. She walked up to one of them. If they were empty, she could keep some of her own clothes in them, as her wardrobes were already overflowing, thought Swadha as she pulled the door handle of one wardrobe. It didn't open. She recollected that they were locked. She picked up her phone to call Haasil and ask for the keys.

This one phone call, Swadha didn't know, was a gigantic wave in the calm ocean of her marriage, which would eventually become impossible to ride.

Pallavi

Pallavi had marked the man. This would be her next mojo in life. Breaking up marriages. Breaking something that was built by people with love and care. For any second person witnessing this, it would make Pallavi plain evil, but in her own mind, she was justified. *Even my love story was hacked by life!* Even the thought of it aroused her sadistic mind. Moreover, she wasn't kidnapping innocent husbands. She would only present herself as a temptation to them. The ones who fell would be the rotten ones who didn't know how to respect loyalty. So, in a way, she was doing a favour to those unaware wives who thought their husbands were a piece of the Almighty. Or so Pallavi told herself.

She had interpreted her heartbreak as a disease given to her by life. And now she was hell-bent on not suffering it alone. She wanted to spread it, turn it into an epidemic, a pandemic if possible. And in the process, Pallavi didn't realize she was slowly becoming a monster whose only humane feature was her love for Haasil. Her Dino. Whom she was still in love with. For only in love can people hate so much. It was embedded right in the last folds of her subconscious that her conscious mind never dared to accept it.

It didn't take her long to get Shalini's husband's name from the reception. Eerav. After Pallavi saw him at the pool, she next saw him during the lunch buffet at the restaurant on the eighteenth floor of the hotel. Shalini was sitting beside him. Pallavi had her eyes on him. His only striking feature was that he was tall. And that he looked younger than Shalini.

A little into lunch, she noticed him eyeing her a couple of times. Especially after she had followed him to the buffet corner, and asked in the silkiest of voices if he could pass her a plate. It was the kind of voice that usually turned men readily servile. Eerav did as asked. Pallavi thanked him—again in the same silky voice—and went to serve herself, knowing well his eyes had to be on her. A slight turn of her head and it was confirmed. That was cue enough for her to take the next step.

When Eerav went up to the dessert section, Pallavi joined him.

'Don't try that. It's ewww!' she said, seeing him pick up a particular dessert.

'Eerav Hinduja,' the man said. Pallavi liked the way he skipped talking about the dessert and came to the point to which she would have otherwise brought him after two more lame dialogues.

'Shivi Mishra,' Pallavi lied and shook hands with him. The smirk on his face, the naughty glimmer in his eyes along with the hard, full-of-intent handshake told Pallavi he was an experienced fish. Perhaps he knew exactly why she was there, advising him about desserts. Men like him, Pallavi thought, are always the perfect husband for their wives. For in their projected perfection, they hide their pervasive imperfections.

She saw Shalini join him, carrying a small dessert plate. Pallavi gave them some distance, collected her desserts on a plate and went back to her seat. Her deduction was ready. This one would be easy, she thought, as she was the water where fish like Eerav thrive.

Her deduction was validated when she saw Eerav and Shalini pass by her seat, with Eerav saying aloud that they were there in the hotel for two nights. Pallavi's experience told her this information wasn't for Shalini.

That very night when Pallavi accompanied Shivi for a drink at the hotel's in-house bar, she wasn't surprised to see Eerav there with Shalini. She took a table opposite them and kept eyeing him. It was time to make it obvious from her end that she was interested. In the next few minutes, Pallavi too was sure about Eerav's intention from the way he returned her look. When Shalini excused herself to go to the washroom, Eerav was quick to come to Pallavi's table.

'Do we know each other?' he asked.

'We can.'

'No, the way you've been eyeing me tells me we know each other.'

'I'm sorry, but I look at interesting personalities that way. The ones whom I personally want to . . . dig.' The last word came out rather seductively. Shivi, who was sitting opposite Pallavi, almost choked on her cocktail.

Eerav glanced at Shivi once. She didn't look at him. Then he looked at Pallavi.

'How about digging me in the morning tomorrow? Say 9 o'clock?'

Pallavi gave her most bewitching smile and said, 'Morning digs are the best.'

'3104.' Eerav said and went back to his table.

'What was that?' Shivi asked, looking shell-shocked.

'His room number,' Pallavi laughed, gulping her vodka.

'I mean, look at his guts! Is that how husbands talk to strange ladies in a bar?' Shivi nibbled on some of the snacks they had ordered.

'My guess was right. Their marriage could be recent, not his cheating ways. In fact, he looks like a pro. And busting pro-balls are a real orgasm for me.' Pallavi finished her drink and gestured to the waiter for a repeat.

'Please don't tell me you're going to his room in the morning,' Shivi said.

'9 o'clock, sharp.' Pallavi noticed Shalini join Eerav at their table. She averted her eyes to Shivi and continued, 'And you'll bring his wife to the room exactly at 9.30 a.m. Sharp.'

A bitchy realization-smile appeared on Shivi's face as she sipped her cocktail, enjoying it like never before.

The next morning, exactly at nine, Pallavi pressed the doorbell of room number 3104. Eerav opened it. He was in a loose tee and tiny shorts. His morning ruffled hair made him look enticing even though he wasn't a traditionally handsome man. Pallavi noticed he had worked-out arms, beefy thighs and a pronounced shoulder line.

'Miss Mishra came right on time, huh?' he said.

'If one doesn't come on time, the climax gets delayed. Why do that?' Pallavi said and entered the room. She had already messaged Shivi to clock her entry.

'Where's she?' Pallavi asked.

'Having her breakfast downstairs,' said Eerav. He removed some of Shalini's clothes from the couch. Pallavi settled on it.

They chit-chatted for five minutes after which both were on top of each other, naked. Like Pallavi, Shivi too was on time. As the doorbell rang, Eerav reluctantly got up as Pallavi moved away from him. He picked up a towel kept on the chair by the study table, wrapped it around his waist and walked up to the door to open it. He saw Shalini standing there, Shivi behind her. The latter gave an acknowledging nod to Eerav and said sarcastically, 'I guess my friend is inside.'

Eerav glanced at Shivi, then at Shalini. By then, Pallavi had appeared behind him; all dressed, with a vixen smile. There was an awkward silence. Nobody moved till Pallavi walked past Eerav and eyeing Shalini said, 'Happy married life.'

As Pallavi and Shivi went back to their rooms, Shalini entered and locked the room door.

'What was that?' she asked Eerav.

'I don't know,' he shrugged.

'The other girl told me there's a surprise for me. Idiot. Anyway, I've told you so many times to keep your fuck buddies at bay when I'm around. Listen . . .' Shalini said, walking to her suitcase. She opened it and turned to look at Eerav.

'I got a call from my husband. He is coming one day earlier. I'll have to leave now.'

'What?' Eerav came close to her. 'You promised two more nights, baby.'

Shalini turned and held his cheeks as if he was her kid. 'I know, but you know how it is. I'll let you know when he is flying out again. And don't complain like a fuck-boy. You already had your extra session. Was she good?'

'Will figure that out soon,' he said and watched Shalini pack and leave the room in no time.

'I'll pay for the room. You don't bother,' were her parting words.

Pallavi was getting ready with Shivi in her room. They were supposed to fly in another three hours but had to report at the airport in an hour.

'I know the husband was an asshole and he needed to be called out,' Shivi said, doing her eye make-up. 'But I still think it's their business. Who are we to sham their marriage?'

Pallavi zipped up her skirt, went to the couch and, while putting on her stockings, said, 'Who cares about what their marriage is. All I know is I've got an infection. I tried my best to heal it. It got worse. Now I love to spread it. And tell myself there's not me alone in this shitty universe suffering from a shitty thing. There are others. It's a group. This realization gives me peace.'

Shivi picked up her lipstick but before applying it said, 'What's this infection? Who gave it to you?'

Pallavi's intimate moments—both emotional and physical—with Haasil flashed in front of her. They made her feel weak for she couldn't do anything to get them back. Did she want them back? Did she want him? Pallavi abhorred such questions. She went to the mini fridge, took out a couple of miniature vodka bottles and gulped them down.

'Bro, we will be on duty soon,' Shivi looked shocked.

They heard the room's doorbell ring.

'Must be the bellboy,' Shivi said. Pallavi went and opened the door. And was surprised to see Eerav.

'Don't you want to finish what you started, Miss Pallavi?' He had a condescending smile for her. Just the kind she despised in men.

Swadha

'Why, what happened?' Haasil asked when he heard his wife inquire about the wardrobe keys. Swadha felt he sounded a little cautious as well. As if this was something she shouldn't have asked him. Or he wasn't ready to hear it from her.

Haasil knew that not telling her about the keys would raise unnecessary doubts, so he did tell her where the keys were. And then waited impatiently for he knew she would call back. And she did. Exactly ten minutes later.

'What's Palki's stuff doing here? Didn't you tell me you got rid of it?' Swadha sounded cross. The first time she was so with him, be it in their professional or personal life. They talked for two minutes, after which Haasil said he had a meeting and hung up. Haasil's answer didn't convince Swadha, though.

It's not only Palki's, he'd said. *Somewhere I'm also entwined in those things though I don't remember much.* More than the confession, what disturbed Swadha was the sight of the wardrobe's contents—all of Palki's belongings. They screamed at her, saying Haasil hadn't moved beyond the shadow of Palki, even with Swadha in his life. That latter part was what hurt her the most for she never knew she had married one person but had to live with two. How could anyone accept that? The entire social and emotional fabric of man was designed to stay with one person. The presence of a third—even if phantasmal—was a world-shaking revelation for Swadha.

As she sulked into a depressed state of mind, Swadha thought her love was not potent enough to make Haasil emotionally comfortable enough so he could walk ahead of his past. But was he even ready to do that? Or did he intend to live with her along with Palki's imaginary presence?

When Haasil came back home that day, they didn't talk about the matter. The chums didn't help her cause. Swadha, anyway, was waiting for him to bring it up. He didn't. Swadha too forwent mentioning it. But it remained within her. And the more it stayed within her, the more her conscious mind marinated it with her disturbed feelings. Did it mean Haasil would never be hers completely? Just as she was his? Now that they were married, why couldn't he be thinking of her all the time? Was it childish to expect this much ownership? Or is belonging wholeheartedly to someone in a relationship just a myth?

The constant mental probing brought along some behavioural changes in Swadha. Something that even she wasn't ready for. Or was conscious of to begin with. Earlier in the office, her focus used to be on her work and Haasil, but now she started mentally noting his proximity with his female PA. His other female colleagues. When she chanced upon him talking on the phone with a smile, Swadha feared it could be some female she didn't know about. Haasil wasn't a womanizer, she knew. But she now knew he could hide things from her. Like he hid Palki's phantasmal presence. It was clear to her that his entirety wasn't about her alone. Her entirety was about him. He was her universe. She wasn't. Not that his actions said anything else. Except there were nights when Swadha sensed him getting up from the bed and spending some time alone inside the room where Palki's things were. He thought Swadha was asleep but she felt nauseated lying in her bed pondering about it all. There was nobody to share such a private update of her life. The breeze of doubt ended up becoming a storm of suspicion. So much so that it propelled Swadha to the extent of putting spyware in Haasil's phone.

Haasil had gone to have a shower one morning when she unlocked his phone. Both knew each other's passwords. She installed the spyware and started keeping a tab on his messages, chats and calls. *Are there more women I don't know about in his life?* Though nothing untoward or suspicious happened on Haasil's part, Swadha went to sleep better at night from then on. It made her falsely believe she had some control over his life. That's one of the ugly facets of a relationship. *You be mine and behave the way I want you to.* The first casualty of being in a relationship, more often than not, is one's individuality. With no proof of any other woman, the only thing that was left to be taken care of was Palki.

One day, when Haasil wasn't at home, she entered Palki's room. She unlocked the wardrobe and stole a brooch of Palki's. She locked the wardrobe, then threw the brooch away. One night later when Haasil entered the room, Swadha was alert. When he came out of the room without realizing the brooch had been removed, Swadha smiled to herself. She had arrived at a solution.

From the next day onwards she either removed small things that one wouldn't register per se and substituted the clothes and cosmetics with their duplicates. She went to obsessive lengths to find the same products on the Internet and order them. Then kept them exactly where the originals were. It was her way of replacing Palki's absence with her presence. From then on, whenever Haasil went into the room at night to spend time with Palki's belongings, Swadha knew he was actually with her. She couldn't help but smile in peace. She had claimed that part of Haasil which was conquered by Palki. It gave her a different kind of orgasm. And calmness.

When Haasil came into their bedroom one night, after having his me time in Palki's room, Swadha initiated their lovemaking, taking control. The situation had made Swadha aware of a dark corner within her that she didn't know existed before. Had Palki been there in person, Swadha would have made her sit tight and watch how she made love to Haasil. Claiming him with every kiss. The dark thought took her by surprise as well. Even the sudden dominant side that she was displaying to Haasil was a revelation. A woman who fights to claim her man is a different creature altogether.

While riding Haasil rather furiously, Swadha glanced at herself in the mirror in front of the bed—for a moment she felt she didn't know the person in the reflection. She was no longer the innocent, coy girl who was hopelessly in love with Haasil. Instead, in the fifteen or sixteen months of marriage, for the first time she could see a conniving lady in her reflection. *Is it my love for Haasil that has altered me? Or is it my desire to make Haasil love me the way I love him that did it?* Swadha closed her eyes and chose to feel the impending climax hit her.

And this time, it broke her from within.

Palki

Life's strange. And its ways stranger. Palki understood it when she became one with many at the construction site without even having to speak the language others were speaking. All she had to do was follow what they were doing. Along with several other women, she too carried the bricks and mortar from one point in the construction site to another on a daily basis from morning to night. At the end of each day, everyone was given some money.

Palki didn't know what others did with the money they received as wages; she saved hers. Every night, she simply went and sat down with some of the women who had set up a small kitchen. People didn't mind her presence. Palki was a non-intrusive person. Her silence was something odd in the constantly chirping group of women. Whenever she went to them at night, someone or the other ended up sharing food with her. In turn she gave them a part of the daily money. It made her famous among the group as an honest and kind soul. Palki, though, didn't understand why goodness was so valued. Wasn't it how things should be with humans? And then she answered herself, thinking perhaps that, like every other valued thing, goodness was rare.

Some of the women did try to talk to her. Owing to her skin colour and features, they understood she wasn't a local. Some thought she was perhaps a foreigner. But none could squeeze any information out of her. Not even her name. Not because Palki didn't want to share. She didn't remember enough to share anything. Palki preferred to remain quiet, reckoning they wouldn't understand her language. The only friend she made was Chiku, a toddler of a couple who worked along with Palki.

One thing that she never shared with anyone was the amount of pain her body suffered every night after the day-long physical activity. She looked around, only to be surprised to see no other woman complaining as such. She realized she was physically weaker than them. Maybe they were used to such intense physical labour all their life. She clearly wasn't.

In spite of the pain, Palki never took any leave. Except for Sundays when the workload was less, Palki used to spend the time wondering about her past. She used to close her eyes and practise thinking back from the time she was dropped at the construction site by the private bus. All she could track back to was the first time she opened her eyes inside Hariharan's hut. Everything before that was still vague. As if someone had cut out that part of her brain where it was all stored. It was during one such helpless night that Palki realized the importance and power of memories. If one is bereft of them, one is bereft of one's own life. One's own self.

One of the private engineering college buildings, whose construction was going on, was half-ready with its sprawling lobby that had some impressive décor. Once while playing with Chiku after work, Palki chased her into the building. She kept calling her till she found herself inside the lobby. When she switched on the lights to see if Chiku had hidden herself there, Palki couldn't help but admire the interiors. The lavish sight seemed to bring back some memories. As if she had lived in such a space before. The lamps, the couch, the chandelier . . . Her wondrous spell was broken by one of the guards who brought in Chiku and asked the two to get out of the lobby. Though she ran off with Chiku, Palki couldn't forget the déjà vu she experienced inside.

Around sixteen months later, Chiku told her, using her cute hand gestures, that they would all be travelling back home. Others seemed happy about it but not Palki. When she went to her tiny space where she used to sleep within the construction site, sleep had deserted her. Palki didn't want to go back. The least she could do was move forward in life. If she had come to this construction site from the forest where she had opened her eyes, all bruised and injured, she believed she could reach a city as well one day. Not that she had any plans how to do it. She did watch city dwellers come to the construction site from time to time. Their dressing sense told her they weren't locals. She even heard them talk in English which she understood. She tried to talk to one of them but the guard didn't let her.

The next day, after months of relentless work, her tired body expressed itself in the form of a high fever. Lying in her space, she noticed people queuing up at some distance happily, to get into a private bus. She saw some women coming for her. Palki somehow managed to get up and went to the other side of the site to hide herself. Not finding her at her space or anywhere nearby, the women had to take a call.

The bus driver was honking away, asking everyone to hurry up. The women decided to return to the bus.

Palki was relieved but before she could think of what she should do next, the weakness made her collapse to the ground unconscious, little knowing that had she taken the bus, she wouldn't have ever met Haasil. After all, life's strange. And its ways, stranger.

Haasil

He didn't express it, neither with words nor by his demeanour, but Haasil knew what Swadha's problem was. And he didn't blame her for it. Had he been in her place, watching her keeping someone alive in her heart after being married to him, he too would have been upset. Angry. Pissed off.

The one major flaw of the human heart was that it demanded monopoly almost like an obvious eventuality of a relationship, Haasil thought. From the time Swadha had called him to ask for the keys to the wardrobe, he knew sooner or later she would come to know of its contents. Lying to her wasn't feasible at this point. Though till then, he had lied about his true intentions of marrying her.

Haasil was emotionally tired of being in love with Palki's absence. On top of that, he didn't remember their love story distinctly but had only heard about it from Nitin since he recovered physically from the accident. How long could one go on imagining someone loved them? Romantic altruism looks good in a book or movie, not for real. He wanted to give himself a reason to move on but wasn't comfortable with the reason coming of his own volition. Swadha's constant advances gave him that reason. *She loves me*, Haasil used to think, *then why can't I submit to that love? Maybe I too shall love Swadha once I let emotional intimacy happen between us.* This was Haasil's thought the night before he finally asked her out for drinks.

When Haasil had come into the other room for the first time after their honeymoon in the Maldives, he sat down quietly and cried amidst Palki's belongings. Swadha was asleep. Haasil cried not because he missed Palki. He cried because somewhere deep within only he knew, even if Palki wasn't alive for him, what he did and why. He had made a comfort zone for himself by taking the best of both worlds. He married Swadha so he could live a normal domestic life, fulfilling his social and sexual needs. While he kept all of Palki's stuff so he didn't feel the need to distance himself from his vague memories of her. Truth be told, Haasil knew this was selfish as he didn't choose Swadha for what she was or for what he felt for her. He chose her for how he wanted to feel for Palki. She was only a tool he used to move on from Palki in his head.

Unknown to Swadha, Haasil had marked every tangible object that belonged to Palki so that he never lost any of it. When he started noticing the marks were missing from the objects, he started having doubts. He was about to raise an alarm when one night, opening his sleepy eyes a bit, he noticed Swadha fidgeting with his phone. He understood what must have happened. And yet he didn't confront her about it.

If she thinks that just because I didn't tell her about Palki's stuff I could also cheat on her, then let her check and confirm that I won't, Haasil told himself. Anyway, he wasn't the disloyal type. Nor did he intend to be. He didn't judge Swadha for her actions even though he was surprised, for he had never associated such behaviour with her. But love makes one do many things: sometimes surprising, sometimes shocking. Does the world know love's a behaviour-altering drug?

One of those nights, after noticing how fast Palki's stuff was being replaced, Haasil stealthily came into Palki's room. He knew Swadha must have been awake but he didn't make it obvious that he knew. After he opened the wardrobe, he remained still as he stared at the stuff—none of which was Palki's. Instead of rage, which he felt initially, now he experienced relief. Someone else had done what he could never do. Take the stuff out of his house. And hopefully his life. He never had the courage or the gumption to do so. Sometimes you know what's best for you but you need someone else to commit the action for you.

That night, for the first time, Haasil didn't weep in Palki's room. After he stepped out of the room, he knew exactly what he had to do next.

The following morning, Haasil took Swadha to the best breakfast place in Singapore. It was in the middle of their sumptuous breakfast that he started to talk.

'I've called an interior decorator to the office today,' he said.

'For what?' Swadha was genuinely surprised.

'For our home. I wanted to redesign the other room,' he stressed the word 'other'.

Swadha's hand stopped just before her lips. Then she kept her spoon on her plate.

'Are you serious?' she asked. She looked like a traveller who had suddenly discovered a destination after years of wandering.

Haasil stretched out his hand to clasp hers.

'Remember, you'd once asked me something?'

Swadha shrugged.

'That what I would do if Palki came back?'

Swadha didn't react but she remembered it well. She had asked him that during one of the post-sex sessions after she had discovered what was in the wardrobe in the other room.

'I didn't answer then. Because I didn't have an answer.' He looked at Swadha reassuringly and continued, 'Now I have an answer.' Haasil half stood up. Leaning forward, he kissed her forehead. It was not only an answer for Swadha. It was sheer relief. She had moist eyes. Finally, she could say goodbye to that insecure side of hers.

'Thank you, Haasil,' she said and meant it. Haasil also intended to thank her. He didn't say it, though.

Pallavi

After a long time, a guy had scored over Pallavi. Not only scored but made a fool out of her. The man whom she thought was the husband was basically the newly married Shalini's lover.

Pallavi realized this when Eerav had come to her room to see if they could finish what they had started in his room. The tone of mockery in his voice told her he was there not for the action, but because he had sized her up. And wanted to have fun at her expense. Though Pallavi had shut the door on his face as a response, she had made up her mind to level the score with him. Or maybe go a notch higher and outscore him. It was a kind of challenge that had never happened before. And the condescending smirk, she would not forget that. How could a man flash her that and be happy? Now that he did, Pallavi swore, this one needed to be destroyed.

Staying at the same hotel for some time now, she had befriended one of the receptionists, Latika. The latter was going through some relationship problems. Three sessions of 'counselling' by Pallavi over drinks had made her feel good. In turn, Pallavi took all of Eerav's information from the reception desk. He was putting up in Mumbai but his residential address on the photocopy of his Aadhaar card read New Delhi. Her den.

The following weekend, Pallavi landed in Delhi. And a day later, she arrived at his address. It was a posh-looking two-storeyed house in Panchsheel Park. The nameplate outside read: Hinduja Home. Pallavi opened the gate herself. Right then a man in a security guard's uniform came running up.

'*Haanji*, madamji,' he said. Looking at her he understood she wasn't any normal sales girl.

'Is Eerav here?' she asked. The guard nodded and showed her in.

Pallavi rang the bell on the main door. It was opened by a female servant, who settled her on one of the couches in the huge hall. The interiors and decor told her she was sitting in someone's home, who had both riches as well as classy taste. A moment later, a lady came out. She looked the sophisticated type.

'I'm sorry, you are here for?'

'Eerav,' said Pallavi.

'Oh.' The woman's expression told her perhaps a girl wanting to meet Eerav was something unusual.

'And this is regarding . . .?'

'I'm his girlfriend,' Pallavi said confidently.

There was genuine happiness on the lady's face. Pallavi found that odd.

'Eerav! Your girlfriend is here,' the lady suddenly spoke up. Instead of him, Pallavi saw three more ladies of varied ages, from a teenager to a young adult to a middle-aged woman, step into the hall with obvious eagerness. Pallavi gave them an unsure smile, standing up. The next moment, Eerav, in casual shorts and a tee, came in. He looked as bewildered as the ladies. He stopped on seeing Pallavi. The latter was beaming from ear to ear.

'Hi, baby!' Pallavi called.

The ladies looked at Eerav—eyes wide—then at Pallavi.

'I'm his mother,' the sophisticated lady who had come in first said. Pallavi rushed to her and hugged her.

'Eerav has spoken so dearly of you, Aunty. Glad to meet you.'

Mrs Hinduja wasn't just impressed. She was floored. *Who was this beautiful and royal-looking girl that her son had kept in the dark this far*, she wondered.

'From when do you know each other?' Mrs Hinduja asked a frozen Eerav.

'Soulmates know each other since their past lives, Aunty,' Pallavi quickly answered.

Eerav, by now, had understood this was her revenge for what he had done to her at the hotel. He had never thought she could be this dangerous. And he also knew if he didn't interrupt then and there, further damage, of the irreversible kind, was in store.

'Just a couple of months,' Eerav lied and came to stand beside Pallavi.

'Damn, I forgot we had to go out today, right?' He turned to Pallavi and made a pleading face.

'I guess so. Why else do you think I'm here?' said Pallavi.

'How can she leave just like that? You haven't even introduced us all,' the middle-aged lady said.

'That's Aditi. That's Aishwarya. That's Ananya. My sisters,' Eerav said in a rush, referring to the teenager, the young adult and the middle-aged lady, respectively.

'Women power!' Pallavi gushed. 'But Aunty, you don't look like you are the mother of four kids.'

This girl is getting better every second, Mrs Hinduja thought and said, 'Thank you, beta.'

'Don't mention it, Aunty. The kind of upbringing your son has got being with so many women shows,' Pallavi shot a sharp glance at Eerav, 'when he is outside.'

Only Eerav sensed Pallavi's sarcasm. He literally held Pallavi by the arm and pulled her towards the main door.

'We are going out now. See you all in the evening.'

'Bhaiya!' the teenager called out. 'Don't you think you want to change your bathroom slippers?' Her face said she'd given up on her brother.

'We aren't going far.'

Eerav didn't stop till he brought Pallavi outside his house and then a little distance into the lane.

'What the fuck are you doing?' Eerav now sounded like the same man who was screwing someone else's wife in the hotel.

'I was here to tell you nobody fucks with Pallavi.'

'Oh, done that? Happy? Now please don't act any smarter.'

'But I think your mother really likes me.'

'Don't push it. Please!'

'Now that we are fair and square, I don't intend to. Goodbye Mr Hinduja. It was lovely fucking you up in a very different way.' She flashed that I-am-superior-to-you smile and added, 'I'm sure you will have a lot to answer the gorgeous, and now hungry in an I-want-to-know-more-about-her way, ladies inside.'

Pallavi strolled to her car and drove past him in the next few seconds.

No, it isn't over, Eerav thought, *but first things first.* How would he answer his family who had seen him with a girl after five years? It would lead to the kind of conversation he loathed. *Yeah, you did fuck me up*, Eerav thought and went in.

Four days later, when Pallavi was relaxing in the bathtub in her room at the Westin, Mumbai, the extension phone pinned on the wall rang.

'Ma'am, there's an Eerav Hinduja who wants to meet you.' A sly smile appeared on her face as she said, 'Please ask him to wait in the café. I'll join him soon.'

Forty-five minutes later, Pallavi joined him. Eerav was already one and a half cups of black coffee down. She sensed his irritation. But to irk the already irked male aroused Pallavi.

'I hope I'm not late,' she said.

'Not at all.' Eerav gave her a tight smile as she settled opposite him. She looked up at the barista who knew her well. She smiled, he smiled, knowing she wanted her favourite frappé.

'So, what brings you here, Mr Hinduja?' Pallavi asked with as much innocence in her voice as she could muster.

Eerav gave her a sharp look and said, 'Let's cut the crap. You couldn't possibly have known I have a family.'

'Oh, that act was completely impromptu. All I wanted was to fuck you up. Seeing the ladies, I knew exactly how I should go about it. I'm good at thinking on my feet, you see.'

'Do you have the slightest idea what hell broke loose on me after you left that day?'

'Tch, tch, tch,' she put on a sympathetic tone and said, 'Is that so? Poor boy.' There was stark mockery in her voice.

'And you flew down to Mumbai to tell me that?' Pallavi shot back. 'Or is it another married woman?'

Eerav didn't respond. That was response enough for Pallavi.

'Your innocence is so delightful right now,' Eerav said with contempt a few coffee sips later.

'You should have thought about that before fucking with me.'

'Excuse me, I didn't fuck with you. You pursued me. And you got what you deserved.'

'Who was the one who came up to my room with that stupid you-messed-with-the-wrong-guy smirk?'

Eerav averted his eyes. He knew she was right. He simply wanted to tease her. No harm. But how was he to know she was a crazy girl who would hound him back to his house in Delhi? Fuck, who does that?

'Anyway, what can I do for you now? You took the trouble of tracking me and then coming over here. I must have raised some hell.' With every passing second, Pallavi was finding the conversation amusing.

'Your act, apparently, was convincing. And the women haven't let me be in peace since. I told them I didn't know you but they think I'm not telling them the truth.'

'What's the truth?'

'That I'm done with girls.'

Pallavi gave him a renewed smile.

'You mean you are gay? What were you doing with Shalini and me then?'

Eerav shook his head in the negative. And was about to speak when the barista brought the frappé.

'Thanks, Vikas,' Pallavi said, glancing at the barista and then looking back at Eerav.

'I'm straight, but I don't want to involve myself with any girl in a serious manner.'

'Ooh la la. A singed heart?'

'Something like that.'

'And to elude her, that one-woman-man which you were once now has become a playboy?' Pallavi was second-guessing.

'Kind of.'

'You don't come across that soft,' Pallavi said. She knew her eyes on him was making him uncomfortable. And that made her enjoy the moment more. Men-in-a-spot was her favourite sport.

'You don't have to be soft to be scarred. Sometimes the impact is too hard. Too intimate. Too intrinsic. And too stubborn to not leave any imprint. Doesn't matter how much you try and rinse yourself within. Excuse me,' Eerav said. She watched him walk to the washroom. That he choked by the last line told Pallavi the scar hadn't healed. By the time he came back, Pallavi had only one question for him.

'What do I have to do now?' She sounded serious. Eerav looked at her as if the person he had left behind when he went to the washroom and the one now were two different women.

The following weekend, Pallavi went to Eerav's home in Delhi for lunch. This time she seemed less flirty. She met his mother and sisters once again and convinced them that she was just a friend of Eerav's and what she'd told them days ago was only a prank. Their faces fell collectively.

It was when Eerav excused himself to attend to a work call that one of his sisters narrated what had happened with Eerav half a decade ago. Listening to her, Pallavi's whole judgement about him changed. And she felt a longing to know him better. That was unprecedented for her. Till then, she felt she alone was 'infected' by life, but now she knew there was someone else too. Her tribe.

It wasn't that what she heard from Eerav's sister was new. A girl breaking a boy's heart wasn't news any more. Pallavi herself had broken so many hearts. It was what became of Eerav after the heartbreak that caught Pallavi's attention.

He tried to kill himself twice in one month. Started consuming insane amounts of alcohol and was mildly into drugs. He was assigned a therapist by his family after which he was in rehab in the US for a year. He came back sober but a different person. His mother heard him cry in the wee hours of the night. When he came out of his room, he seemed all right. Or perhaps it was his defence against the internal turmoil. His sister told Pallavi that they understood he didn't want to disturb them with his personal story so he kept pretending to be all right in front of them.

Something in the story mirrored Pallavi's own emotional state. She hadn't been to any rehab but only she knew what a mess she had been for years now. Being an alcoholic was common ground. There was a small emotional vacay when she experienced the time of her life living with Haasil. But that was more of an illusion which she had assumed as reality. When the bubble burst, she was way more acidic, edgy and broken than ever before. And broken people have a cosmic blessing to identify equally broken souls. Pallavi had identified Eerav through his sister's narration.

Though after she left his place, Eerav had messaged her a 'thank you', Pallavi knew they would meet again. She followed him on Instagram. It took two hours for him to accept her into his private account. She noticed his account was full of photographs of people, places and animals. None of his own. Pallavi quietly kept a track of his posts and stories. On the thirty-seventh day, she saw his story with a location tag of Jaipur where he was putting up.

Pallavi was in Delhi and had two consecutive rest days before her next flight. She drove down to Jaipur and checked into the same hotel that Eerav had tagged himself on his Instagram story. She took a cold bath, then relaxed till it was night. She called the reception and inquired about Eerav. She was given the room number. She decided to knock on his door.

Eerav opened the door, looking distressed. He had put up the 'Do Not Disturb' tag. But one look at Pallavi and he didn't know what to say.

'Hey,' Pallavi said with a smile. She noticed his eyes were teary. She remembered what his sister had told her about his sporadic crying rituals.

'Hey!' Eerav smiled back, trying to change his emotional gear. It didn't work with Pallavi.

'Let's have coffee downstairs?' she asked. Pallavi knew she had to give him some time to sort himself out. Now that she knew who he really was, she couldn't take his pretence.

'Yeah, sure,' Eerav said.

Fifteen minutes later, they were sitting opposite each other in the hotel café.

'All right, the obvious first,' Eerav said. 'Am I being stalked?'

'Of course,' Pallavi said with her trademark smirk.

Eerav leant close to her and whispered, 'Is it about my trying to take my life?' He reclined and added, 'If it is, then I don't regret it one bit. This life anyway sucks.'

Pallavi waited for him to sip his coffee and then said, 'I had a talk with your sister when I was at your place. I know more about you than you know.'

Eerav's visage changed a little. It seemed he understood what she had said but was unsure how to react.

'Was it necessary to know? I mean how did it help you?' he asked.

'She narrated, I listened.'

'And now you are here to sympathize with me?'

'I'm here for myself, not you.'

Eerav frowned.

'I'm as broken and as scarred as you.' There was a slight choke in her voice. She preferred to cover it up with a sip of her black coffee.

The confession took Eerav by surprise. By then he'd put Pallavi within the opinion capsule of being a rich, shallow, brattish girl who had nothing better to do in life than probe into other people's lives just for a thrill.

'So, do we give each other a shoulder?' Eerav asked.

'I have a proposal,' Pallavi said.

'I'm listening.'

'I'll tell you about it but before that, I want to check something.'

Eerav frowned inquiringly.

Sometime later, Eerav found himself leaving with Pallavi in her car out of the hotel. Near the outskirts of Jaipur, she parked on the side of the express highway where the traffic was rather busy. Pallavi was carrying two bottles of Ketel One vodka.

'You sure about this?' Eerav asked. When he heard about it from her, something inside him felt charged up. Pallavi nodded. She started drinking from her bottle. He took the other bottle from her and sipped from it while looking at the vehicles vrooming past across the highway.

Once they had emptied their bottles, they gave each other that punch-drunk glance, a half smile and then, stepping out of the car, they started walking on the busy highway.

Pallavi's bet was, if they survived, he was meant to hear and enact her proposal for him. He had agreed.

Palki

P alki was told that she had been unconscious for two days.
When she opened her eyes, she felt weak but the fever had
worn off. She was still at the construction site. She noticed a
different set of people, families setting up their kitchens and
small tents to live in. *Was she destined to be here forever?* she wondered.

The first thing Palki did after gaining consciousness was
to check the place where she used to hide her money. It was a
small hole in the ground which she had dug seeing one of the
women previously working there do that. Palki had covered
the hole with a stone. She was relieved to find it as she had left
it. Later, recuperating from the fever, she decided to work for
some more months till she had enough money saved to make
a move to the city.

This time, instead of a toddler, a young lady, Sumati,
became her friend. Sumati was six months pregnant, yet
she did as much work as the others. The common ground
between the ladies was that Sumati used to speak broken
Hindi. One day, while relaxing together after work hours,

she told Palki that she had learnt Hindi from her first husband who was from UP. He had died in an accident after which she remarried, to a local from her village. He used to work in a hotel in the city. The mention of the city made Palki request Sumati if she could meet her husband once he came to visit her. Sumati assured her that he was coming two months later to take her to the city. Palki could accompany them then. Since then, Palki was only counting the days. Not that she knew exactly what she was going to do in the city, but those few minutes in the lobby and the déjà vu feeling she carried thereafter told her she belonged to the city.

A month later, Sumati took a day off. So did Palki. Together, they went to a nearby fair where loads of people from nearby villages had also come. It was their annual fair. People were busy either playing little games or shopping at the flea market or having different delicacies from the stalls. Most of the kids were enjoying the giant wheel experience.

Palki bought a few handmade dolls for herself. Traipsing in the fair, she noticed a man by an open stall who was doing permanent marking on people's skin. Most of them were getting their names inked on their arms. She recollected, for the umpteenth time, she had one such mark on her skin too. *Palki-Haasil*. On her hip. Were they her parents' names? Or siblings? Or was one of them her name and the other . . .? Were they even related? Palki frowned. She went into a sitting area made of bricks. There was a buzz all around but she suddenly felt empty within.

'Hold it, please.'

She looked up to see a man with a camera around his neck. He didn't look like anyone from a nearby village. Or even a local. At that point, Palki didn't know the man was her ticket to escape to a better present. A present where she wouldn't be alone. Haasil too would be there with her.

Swadha

The first thing Swadha had done after Haasil informed her about his moving on from Palki, was remove the spyware from his phone. She didn't confess about its presence in his phone either, wondering what would he think of her if she did.

The following weekend, she was in one of the best bistros of Singapore, Gardens by the Bay, with Haasil, hogging on a delicious Sunday brunch, when she noticed someone familiar. It took some time for Swadha to recognize her college mate Arpita. She used to be a reserved, coy girl from a small town who had come to Delhi for her graduation. The Arpita who sat at a table in front of her had short hair with a burgundy tinge on one side. Plus multiple piercings along with three visible tattoos and a bohemian vibe to her. The next minute, Arpita's eyes caught Swadha's. She recognized her and came to her instantly.

'Hey, Swadha! What a surprise,' Arpita said.

'Indeed.' Swadha couldn't help but check out her belly piercing popping out of her crop top.

They shared a warm smile after which Swadha introduced her to Haasil. They started talking about their graduation time and the whereabouts of their other batchmates. Haasil excused himself, saying he would rather leave the two friends to themselves. He left for home. Arpita shifted to Swadha's table and they continued their brunch.

The girls kept recollecting one incident after another. When Arpita heard Swadha and Haasil's love story, she was beyond shocked with the turns it had taken.

'That's why I believe relationships are all destined,' Arpita quipped.

'Enough of me now. What's up with you? Give me the deets,' Swadha said. She sounded a bit like one of those family aunts who hog gossip for mental calories. She didn't mind being so intrusive for that's the hallmark of an old-friends meet.

Arpita took a deep breath as if she was bracing herself and then said, 'Don't know where to begin. Ritesh and I were so much in love. Like we were dating since we joined Birlasoft.'

'That was your campus placement, right?'

'Yeah, first job. First proper relationship. Everything was hunky-dory. We went on vacays together. Lived-in for some time. Then got married. After three years, I started feeling Ritesh was not his old self. Like there was this restraint in him. Our intimacy also suffered. And then I discovered that he was having an affair. I did confront him. You know what he said?'

Swadha had stopped eating by then. Her ears and eyes were all on Arpita.

'He said that I wasn't caring enough. I wasn't giving him enough attention and thus he felt the need for someone else in his life. How does one quantify this "enough" care and "enough" love? I understood this is shit which only men can pull up. I asked him to . . .'.

The rest of it Swadha did hear but her mind was somewhere else. A fierce insecurity gripped her. *Was she caring enough for Haasil? Was he happy enough with her? What if . . . he too . . .* Swadha cringed at the thought. Before the dream-like twist happened in her life, of Haasil proposing and marrying her, Swadha could still live on assuming Haasil could only be a desire of hers. But now she was married to him. Already had memories with him which she wouldn't ever sever from herself until death. If Haasil left her then . . . the sinking feeling in her stomach told her she should not dare think that. Swadha left the bistro swearing to herself she wouldn't allow such crap to creep into her marriage.

She decided to up her gear as far as her attention to Haasil was concerned. While doing so, she crossed one cardinal line that should ideally not be crossed in any relationship. Even if two people are a couple, they have the right to their own individuality. A relationship is a collective but without a compromise on one's individualism.

Haasil started having less of his own personal space. A space where he wanted to be with himself. 'Me time' in millennial jargon. Every time Swadha felt he was alone, she accompanied him. Though the intention wasn't bad, the outcome didn't taste great. Especially to Haasil. An irritation started to brew inside him. If life was divided into camera frames, there was not one single frame he was living without Swadha. Does loving someone really mean so much of togetherness? Sometimes, Haasil realized, constant presence can also be toxic. As days passed, he felt he had become someone who was living for the relationship alone. Not for himself. Whereas the truth was that Haasil had married Swadha for himself, not because he was head over heels in love with her.

One night, like so many other nights, Haasil was watching a late-night football match on television. Every alternate minute, Swadha was checking to see if he needed anything. Haasil patiently answered for some time. Then the team he was supporting—Manchester United—started losing. The fallout of this was his bad mood. And the constant probing from Swadha ensured he blew his lid.

It was their first proper fight. Not an ugly one. But the first time he had raised his voice against her. Also, for the first time, Haasil went and slept alone in the other room. For the first time, a silence crept into their relationship in the days that followed. And Swadha wondered if it was the beginning of the end of her 'honeymoon' with Haasil.

Pallavi

A highway police patrol van had spotted the two drunks walking on the highway amidst speeding vehicles. As one of the constables reached them, it didn't take them much time to understand that both were drunk. But they weren't drunk driving. They were drunk walking. *Is there a law against that?* the constable asked his senior.

The senior made the constable frisk the two after which they found Eerav's driving licence in his wallet. And a hotel room key. They went to the hotel, where he was putting up as well, and learnt Pallavi, too, was putting up there. They simply handed the two to the hotel staff who ushered them to their respective rooms. For the police, these were two mental cases. And they had other important things to take care of. It was in the early afternoon that Pallavi knocked on Eerav's door.

'Oh, you too are alive,' Eerav said, seeing her at the door.

'You remember anything?' she asked, marching inside.

'Last thing I remember was following you on the highway. Bro, why the fuck are we alive?' He closed the door and joined her, sitting on the bed opposite her.

'That was the whole point of walking drunk. Do we live or don't we?'

'And because we are alive, you take it as validation for whatever proposal you had in mind?'

'Not really validation. But I just wanted to know if associating with you is worth it or will it be doomed. And if we died or were injured, it would have meant we were doomed. My own exclusive, not yet patented, litmus test against life, you can say.'

'Litmus test against life? I think there's also another word for it. Stupidity.'

'Living on the edge, maybe?' Pallavi lifted her legs up on the bed and, adjusting herself to a more comfortable pose, said, 'Now about the proposal I had in mind.'

'Sure, go ahead.' Eerav took a pillow on his lap. 'I really want to know what divine purpose it is for which we risked life and defied death.'

'I think our wounds are the same. More importantly, what the wounds turned us into. That's also the same. We are wound-twins of sorts.'

Eerav made an I-like-that-term face and continued to listen.

'After I went back from your house pondering about whatever your sister told me about your rehab shit and all, I understood sleeping with married women wasn't just a kick for you. You do so because you want to tell that someone who has invaded your head and heart that you don't give a fuck. But only you know how much of a fuck you give. Same with me.'

Eerav didn't show it, but he was surprised at Pallavi's correct deduction of him. He knew only a wound-twin, as she put it, could have deduced it this way.

'So, what's the deal?' he asked.

'The fact that you didn't protest tells me I was fucking right.' Pallavi had a proud smile. Eerav gave her a tight I-am-not-interested-in-massaging-your-ego smirk.

'I think time has turned us both into a messed-up ball of complications. Earlier, I used to think an untangling wasn't possible. And hence, I started living on the edge. It made me feel my own wounds the least. But meeting you and knowing your backstory, which kind of helped me to see myself from a third person's perspective, I believe the kind of wounds that we both are carrying can heal if we can relay it to someone who is our mirror. You getting me?'

Eerav nodded.

'I propose we become each other's personal diary. You be my ears, I'll be yours. No sex, no possessiveness, no opinions, no judgements and all honesty. Brutal honesty, if need be.'

'A human diary, you mean? Interesting.' *The inner mess is indeed tiresome,* Eerav thought to himself, then said, 'You think it will work out?'

'Let's not even have the pressure of having it work out. Let's just see how it flows.'

'But is it easy to open up in front of a stranger just like that?'

Pallavi stood up, came round to Eerav and whispered, 'We aren't strangers, Eerav. We are two individuals connected via the same wounds. That makes us a tribe.'

As their eyes remained linked, Pallavi whispered again. This time with a question, 'So, in or out?'

Haasil-Swadha

The fight was a major trough in their marriage. What Swadha had not anticipated was the ripples it had. And how those ripples affected their everyday interaction. It was only after the fight that Swadha discovered the egoistic side to Haasil. She was confused about how exactly she should handle it.

Whatever Swadha had heard from other women till date, be it in college or later in the office, they emphasized that it was always their boyfriends or husbands who made up with them after every fight. The more she heard it, the more it became a generalization in her conscious mind. It made Swadha believe that it was one of those gender things that had been normalized at a societal level. That males apologized after fights. Women maintained their expected high-handedness about the matter.

But what she noticed in Haasil post the fight, was a contradiction to the generalization. He didn't look the apologetic type even though her probing came from a place of concern for him. From the next day onwards, Haasil went about his daily routine as if nothing had happened and yet his anger was palpable. He didn't talk much during breakfast or during their morning drive to the office together. He didn't have lunch with her either. He didn't even return her look much, making her feel almost invisible in the office. Professionally, however, he was conversing without any hiccups.

After three days, the same Swadha who was waiting for him to apologize, thinking the fight could have been avoided and Haasil was being kiddish, was now craving to talk to him, to bring back the normality between them. To go back to how they were living before. His monosyllabic responses were irking her. She was ready to apologize as well but the tiny ego in her wasn't letting her take the first step. She simply wanted him to take half a step and she would surrender. But that was not to be.

On the fifth day, around 1 a.m., both of them were lying in bed. That's when she felt his first touch. On her navel under her nightdress. His hand quickly went down inside her panties and started stroking her waxed vagina. For the first few seconds, Swadha was stiff. She was deciding if it was for real or if her horniness was playing a trick on her. Then she eased out, turned and grabbed Haasil's penis. It was erect. For her. It made her wet. In the thin darkness, they turned to look at each other, continuing to masturbate the other. The act was sexual but their eyes were having an ego fight.

Why don't you simply say sorry? It's not a big deal, Haasil's eyes told hers.

If it's not, then why don't you say sorry? her eyes responded.

I was waiting for you.

Same here. I thought the fight wasn't necessary.

Maybe it wasn't. But it happened. So, now what?

You tell me. I wasn't the one to fight.

Swadha felt his fingers probing her G-spot vehemently now. Her grip on his penis weakened as she started moaning. She reached a climax first. Then she made sure he reached his in no time. After cleaning themselves up, they cuddled up for a good night's sleep. No talk. Swadha interpreted the whole action as a truce. She was right and wrong.

Swadha went back to her normal self, going the extra mile to take care of Haasil in every which way she could, but she started sensing a simmering irritation from his side. As if he wasn't enjoying her presence. As if he had connected to a space bereft of her presence and that made him more comfortable. Weirdly enough, he didn't seem to welcome her care and concern. They had another fight.

This time it was propagated by Swadha when she had planned a Saturday night dinner while Haasil wanted to be alone sipping wine. The coldness of this fight went on for a fortnight. Swadha started feeling as if Haasil enjoyed the post-fight aloofness more than her care for him. Every night before sleeping, she started analysing the situation in her mind. And in the end, after three weeks, she came to the conclusion that even if two people were in a relationship, they still need to feed the individual that they were with their own preferences. And those preferences may not align with what they as a couple preferred. There was nothing wrong with that, she thought. This was what Haasil had blasted out during their first fight. Back then, she thought it was ridiculous. Now she knew better.

The thought kept reverberating within her. Two months later, she found a solution.

'Why don't we put this Singapore office on autopilot, bring in a managing director and shift to our New Delhi office? I shall be closer to my family and other friends. Else this work routine is getting to me,' Swadha proposed while they were having dinner.

Haasil thought about it. From the time the first fight had happened, he was in two minds. Every couple had a certain boundary beyond which their peace as a couple was disturbed. Haasil thought Swadha's overt obsession to take care of him was stepping over the line. The only reason he didn't confront her about it was because he thought there was a possibility she would misunderstand him and things would spiral downwards for them if that happened. Maybe Haasil didn't love her the way she loved him but he did care for her. There was an emotional affinity keeping which as a base he had proposed to her. But the constant intrusion into his privacy was something that had gotten on his nerves. He never questioned her love for him, but had started to have issues with the expression of her love. His response to the first fight was more of a subtextual signal to her to not repeat it. Unfortunately, she didn't understand. Haasil chose ignorance as a solution from the second fight onwards. He stopped giving importance to her presence all the time. If that had made her come up with the idea of shifting places, he was happy about it.

Haasil thought about it further over the weekend. It made total sense. In Singapore, neither of them had any personal life or friends. Whenever both went out to party or dinner or even invited people for brunch at their place, they were all professional connects trying for a superficial personal bond. Perhaps once they had their friends back in their lives, Swadha wouldn't keep him as her centre of being all the time. And that would iron out the relationship as well.

Three months later, their tickets to New Delhi were booked. And they began to wrap up their stay in Singapore.

Pallavi

She was in Delhi for one night. And she had to catch up with him before flying off the next morning.

Eerav was supposed to visit a friend's exhibition. He asked her to come along. They would catch up over drinks after the event. Pallavi was game.

'I made him wear a paper mask where I'd written his name,'

Pallavi said. She was sitting beside Eerav, who was driving.

'Why would you write his name on a mask when he was right there with you?' Eerav found the entire thing weird. He had guessed from her message two evenings ago when she had told him excitedly that she wanted to share an incident. It had been some time since they had become each other's human diary. And contrary to what Eerav first thought, it was going rather smoothly. At least he had rediscovered his work focus after a long time.

'I meant I wrote Haasil's name on the paper mask.'

Eerav looked at her and then smirked, pushing on the accelerator. 'Now I want to know more.'

'Rode him. Slapped him. Throttled him. Everything I wanted to do to Haasil.'

By then, Eerav knew who Haasil was and how he had affected Pallavi. Rather, altered her.

'It gives you pleasure, right? Role-playing about taking control over him?'

'I wouldn't say I did it so much for pleasure as I did it to reduce the pain he caused. Imagine you are a place. People come to you for your innocence and scenic beauty. Then an earthquake takes place, which shakes you from within. You may look almost the same as you did before, but only you know how much of yourself you've lost within. And all your life you try to seek that lost thing without knowing what it is and fully knowing you'll never get whatever it is. He had done that to me. Placed me right in the middle of an emotional paradox.'

'But don't you think that by doing all this, you are somewhere keeping him alive inside you? And the more he is alive, the more the wounds he gave you would remain fresh as well?' What Eerav said seemed applicable to his own case as well. And that's what he appreciated about this human-diary thing. He too was able to see himself as a third person while asking Pallavi questions about her choices.

Pallavi pressed the button to slide her window down. She pulled out a cigarette, lit it and took a contemplative drag.

'I won't lie to you. You know, it's been more than a decade. I think I've entered the most dangerous phase now. Of living alongside the wound, the scar, the pain. I've made a home around it. And I realized it when my parents made me meet this guy for a proposal.'

'At least you spared one guy,' Eerav said in a funny tone. Pallavi gave him a sharp glance.

'Feeling light after ages. And that too without an orgasm,' she said.

Eerav gave her an I-know-what-you-mean smile and said, 'You intend to live like this forever? Slapping men with a Haasil face mask on while bedding them? Or will you find different ways of defining your living-on-the-edge existence?'

The way Pallavi turned to look at him, it was clear she wasn't expecting this question. Eerav thought he had stepped across a line.

'Egging you on. Just doing my human-diary job.' His smile was met by Pallavi's.

'I don't know,' she said. 'Maybe, maybe not. I would rather take one day at a time. And react to how I feel about it. If a day comes where I feel detached from all this, probably I shall move on. Else I won't. I mean I'm not really complaining about the mess that my life is because of that man.'

'That's because you have found solace in this mess. Exactly what you meant when you said you have made a home around your wounds.'

'Exactly.'

There were a few minutes of silence.

'Let me be the diary now,' Pallavi said, taking another drag on her cigarette. 'Mouth zipped, all ears.'

Eerav began immediately, as if he had been waiting for his turn.

'I don't know if it's normal or not, but one thing I keep going back to is what was it that broke me within, being in a relationship with her.' Eerav began by reminiscing about his ex.

'After a lot of introspection, running the relationship like a film in my mind for hours, for days and for weeks, I realized

I was actually routine for her. The realization that you can be insignificant for that someone who is the world for you is so painstakingly damaging.' Eerav overtook two cars at one go.

'So it's her treatment of you that damaged you?'

'Irreversibly, I think. Especially when in return I had surrendered everything to her. It made me stop believing that I could actually be special for someone. Anyone.'

'Didn't you feel like killing her?'

'No.' Eerav glanced at Pallavi, then averted his eyes back to the road. 'Unlike your case, I was more focused on what happened to me than what she did to me. Hope I'm making sense.'

'An elaboration would help.' Pallavi took a hard drag, finishing off the cigarette.

'People come into your life. You give your everything assuming that's what the other person will also be giving to maintain the "us" that the two of you have created. And then, you learn that you gave your reality but what she gave was only an illusion. Nothing of what she promised actually happened.'

'Why do you think she did this?' Pallavi didn't know his ex's name. He didn't say, she didn't ask.

'Maybe she already knew whom she was going to get married to. All she needed was a last tango before marriage. And she had it. She was in a long-distance relationship with her fiancé. This, of course, I learnt much later. And she utilized this time to have another man in the city who would be there whenever she wanted him to. I'm not judging her here. Just telling you what I think happened. And then when the time came, she, to my face, asked me to mind my own life.' Eerav brought the car to a slow halt. They had reached the exhibition venue.

Pallavi and Eerav stepped out. Eerav handed the car key to the valet. As he drove the car to the parking lot, they entered the exhibition centre.

'You went into a trip of your own after that?' Pallavi wasn't done with his story yet.

'None of it was wilful like yours. I reacted viscerally to what was happening. Alcohol seemed to numb me. I started consuming more of it. But I don't know if I ever will be able to collect the self-respect which she so easily chopped into pieces. I mean, she could have at least told me she was trying to live something temporarily and then it would have been up to me to choose to partner her in this temporary vacation of hers. In fact, that's what I was for her. A human vacation.'

They stepped into an elevator.

'That's interesting. Bored of your normal life or partner, get another human into your life via some app or something, make a new identity, have whatever you want to have and then boom, gone!'

'That's anyway happening a lot all the time. In the name of loneliness and . . .'

The elevator brought them to the floor where the exhibition was being held. They stepped out.

'Guess what? I've done that to a lot of men myself. My intention and what I got out of it were totally different,' Pallavi said. 'And perhaps you trying to bed married women was your lame way of saving your butchered self-respect and laminating it with false ego.'

'Yeah.'

They entered the exhibition hall. Both wished the conversation could go on but knew it would after an hour. Pallavi saw a man come and hug Eerav. It was Mahesh, Eerav's friend whose photo exhibition it was. Eerav introduced him to Pallavi. She noticed a slight frown on his face when he saw her. Then he excused himself, catering to other guests who were steadily walking in. Meanwhile, Eerav and Pallavi ventured further into the hall, checking out the photographs on display on the four walls.

Ten minutes later, Pallavi realized a lot of the guests present were giving her strange looks. She found it weird. Trying her best to ignore them, she kept walking beside Eerav till they reached a particular photograph on one of the walls. It was of a woman. A facial profile photograph. And looking at it, Pallavi understood why everyone at the exhibition was giving her strange looks. They thought she was the woman in the photograph.

Only Pallavi knew who the woman could possibly be.

* * *

BOOK 2: The Set-Up of Love
(21 Months Later)

Chapter 1

It was Haasil who had filed Swadha's name for a prestigious business award nomination two months ago, without telling her about it. Whatever their personal relationship graph was, nobody could debate with Haasil how much value Swadha had added to his consulting firm. Not because she was married to the co-founder of the firm but she had all the promise, qualifications and acumen one needed for the job. Her performance had ascended even after her role was majorly diversified in recent times.

Swadha came to know about the nomination only when she received an official email inviting her, along with Haasil, for the award show. Her nomination had featured in the top three. One of the three would be awarded in the ceremony. The moment she saw the email, Swadha rushed to his cabin.

'Is this for real?' She put her iPad right in front of him.

'I guess so.' Haasil had an amused look on his face. He didn't even look at the iPad to see what it was. He too had received the same email minutes back. Swadha understood it was his doing. She leapt on to him and gave him a hard, sloppy peck.

'Thanks, love.'

'You deserve this and the award as well, baby.' Haasil kissed her cheeks. Less sloppier than hers.

'When is the award show?' Haasil asked.

Swadha checked her email once again and said, 'Oh my god, it's tomorrow, 8 p.m. onwards.'

'Yeah, so? There's time. We don't have any important meeting tomorrow.' Haasil didn't understand the worry in her voice.

'We have to shop. Did you see who the chief guest is? It's the finance minister himself.' Swadha was excited.

Haasil thought for some time and then called in his PA, Nancy.

'Book two tickets to Dubai tonight. And back tomorrow afternoon.'

Swadha gave him a surprised shrug.

'The best is going to win tomorrow so we have to shop from the best place to look our best.'

Swadha didn't make it obvious but she did 'touch wood' on Haasil's table. And then glanced at him while he was talking to Nancy. She could fall in love with this man just about any time, she thought. And this realization came after some rough sailing in Singapore. No complaints though, Swadha thought. Especially in the last few months, she had sensed a renewed love for her in his actions. Haasil had started taking the initiative unlike what he had done in Singapore or even after their first fifteen months in Gurugram.

The Dubai trip wasn't only about shopping from the best place there. They put up at one of the royal suites in Atlantis, The Palm. They were exhausted by the time they checked-in. They preferred heading for a hot shower right away.

When she saw Haasil stripping and wrapping a towel around his waist, she understood he would join her. She didn't remember the last time they had showered together. Or even made love. Marriage was a funny concept. It gave the much-needed proximity and intimacy a human desires from the core, but after a certain time, the human takes that particular proximity and intimacy so much for granted that he or she never indulges in it. A portion of their mind knows they can have it whenever they want it, yet they rarely experience it. Swadha and Haasil had stepped into that phase in the last six or seven years of their marriage.

After spending an hour in the bathtub together, with his touch tingling her just the way it did when they had honeymooned years ago, they stepped into the rain shower area, naked.

Her hand was on the shower knob when she heard Haasil say, 'Don't turn on the shower.' He left Swadha wondering as he moved out. He came back half a minute later. He was carrying an open bottle of champagne.

'Where are the glasses?' Swadha asked.

Haasil's response was swift. And it wasn't with words. He held Swadha in one strong arm and poured the champagne over her bosom. As it trickled down her breasts, he tasted the champagne, sucking on her, by then, erect nipples. There was instant gooseflesh. The next lot of champagne was poured on her navel. Haasil bent down, slightly pushing his tongue inside her belly button. She couldn't help but hold his hair tight. A moan escaped her mouth. She felt his tongue go down till it reached her vagina seconds after the champagne found its way there. He bent further down, pulling her vaginal lips with his mouth. Swadha didn't know for how long Haasil was giving her oral pleasure. When he stood up, she noticed, the bottle was half empty.

Haasil flipped her, pushed her against the wall and poured the remaining chilled champagne on her nape. He watched it travel to her tail bone. Just when Swadha's skin was used to the champagne's chill again, she felt Haasil's warm tongue on her back. He drew an H with it. The way he used to during the first phase of their marriage. She felt as though Haasil was rediscovering her body.

Till then Swadha had safely concluded that they had perhaps settled into that monotonous phase of marriage where neither makes an extra effort in the relationship, where both take the other for granted and there isn't any newness to be explored. Haasil's actions surprised her. In the last two or three months, Haasil was visibly taking the initiative in their marriage when Swadha least expected it. Whatever the reason, Swadha neither probed nor complained. She wasn't sure which one gave her greater pleasure, though: the way his tongue swirled on her back or the fact that she had got her husband back the way she always wanted?

Once Haasil emptied the champagne bottle on Swadha, he lifted her up and carried her out of the shower room. They made love on the couch, overlooking the Dubai cityscape, for an hour. After which they finally showered their sweaty bodies together. When your lover explores your body it is pleasurable but, in that moment Swadha realized, what's more pleasurable is when your lover, after making love to your body, still makes you feel it's the first time he is exploring it. It made her feel painfully wanted and terribly desired. A feeling she had accepted, perhaps in the months following their shift to Gurugram, she wouldn't be feeling again. For lust is a perishable entity. The more you use it for someone specific, the more you diminish it. Unlike love. Its scope is as gigantic and as mysterious as the universe itself.

After the shower, they slept like babies. They went shopping the next day, ending up buying an Armani tuxedo for Haasil and a gorgeous Dolce & Gabbana dress for Swadha. While heading for Dubai International Airport later in the afternoon, Swadha expressed her anxiety.

'With all this pampering, now I'm feeling the pressure. What if I don't win?'

'Well, in that case, at least we discovered a new way of having champagne,' Haasil winked. Swadha couldn't hide her blushes. She realized that, unlike love, lust ages. And being with Haasil in the shower the previous day, Swadha had understood, a certain unpredictable naughtiness between a couple kept the lust for the other young.

The award show was a gala affair. It was covered by all the leading media channels. There was a red carpet for the arriving guests where they were supposed to pose for media clicks and then give some bites.

Wearing six-inch stilettoes that matched her dress, and for the first time standing half an inch taller than Haasil, Swadha stepped on to the red carpet with him, hand in hand. They stopped for some media pictures, then stood in front of a bouquet of mics. They felt like film stars with all the lights and cameras aiming at them.

'Congrats on your nomination. Anything you would like to say?' asked one of the journalists.

'At the cost of sounding cheesy, I think I can now safely say I reverse the adage that behind a successful man there's a woman. At least in my case,' Swadha glanced at Haasil. He squeezed her hand as she said, 'There's a man. My man.'

After giving some more bites, they walked in. They were ushered into the banquet hall of the five-star hotel. And were given a round table where other nominees were seated with their respective friends, colleagues and family. They met Nitin and Sanjana there, already seated. After the initial hugs, all settled down.

The show began with a stand-up stint from the country's leading comedian after which the awards were announced by the emcee and given away by distinguished guests from various fields. When it came to the award where Swadha was nominated, it was supposed to be given by a veteran Bollywood actor. He stepped on to the podium as the emcee welcomed him. Then opened the envelope which he had carried with him. Swadha could almost hear her heart beat hard. The winner was announced. But she didn't hear anything. Looking at Haasil hooting for her, Swadha understood she had won. They shared a quick hug. She stood up, shared hugs with Nitin and Sanjana and then went to the stage, visibly nervous. She accepted the award from the actor.

Haasil, meanwhile, was recording her winner's speech on his phone. He was beaming from ear to ear. And in between he noticed a WhatsApp message had entered from a name that he had saved on his phone as Akshita Jha.

The message read: *I'm missing you.*

Only Haasil knew Akshita was . . . Palki.

Chapter 2

The shift to Gurugram, eventually, did work in her favour. Or so Swadha kept telling herself every time she saw Haasil at peace once they had settled here. More so in the last two or three months. One look at him and anyone could say he was in a happy place in life. Seeing him happy, Swadha was happier. It wasn't Singapore alone they had left, she thought, but all the bad vibes around their marriage as well.

They had put up at a rented duplex to begin with in Gurugram right after flying down from Singapore. Two months later, Haasil purchased a duplex in the same society. Their company was working from an office floor in one of the DLF towers in Cyber Hub. The most soulful update of their life was that Nitin—Haasil's best buddy and business partner—was there to welcome them in the city. Nitin and Sanjana had married a couple of months after Haasil and Swadha's wedding.

Not all was warm between Haasil and Nitin after Pallavi had stormed into Haasil's life in the past, ushered in by Nitin, and left Haasil in emotional ruin when the truth dawned. The two men had not had a talk regarding the matter. All Nitin knew was that Haasil was deeply hurt. More with him than Pallavi. For he had trusted him after the accident. Though Nitin's intention to bring Pallavi into Haasil's life, and make her play Palki, was to protect Haasil from an irreversible catharsis at that moment in time. The doctor had clearly stated to Nitin, back then, that the news of Palki's supposed demise was potent enough to trigger a fatal consequence in Haasil. Nitin had justified himself in his mind about Palki's substitution with Pallavi but now all that was in the past. He was genuinely happy seeing Haasil finally move on in life.

Shifting to Gurugram, both Haasil and Nitin realized that their souls, perhaps, were waiting with outstretched hands to accept the other; they were just waiting for their physical bodies to turn up. And once they did, the old camaraderie simply flowed.

Haasil was happy to reconnect with Nitin and a few other friends of theirs. Swadha wasn't far behind. She too intentionally reached out to her friends on social media who were in the city. And with time, it had become an unsaid thing between Haasil and her: he would socialize with his friends alone while she would do so with hers. No criss-crosses. Rarely did their acquaintances cross paths. What took Swadha by surprise was learning what a little space in a relationship could do to a couple. Their marriage, now, was akin to a tree spreading its branches and giving them much-needed shade. But it was also keeping them away from the sun for far too long. The little space that they decided to give each other brought the much-needed sunshine into their relationship. Swadha had a refreshing realization: it's not togetherness that repairs a relationship. Perhaps it's a little distance, a little space that does.

The two most important punctuations of a couple's connection are the silences and the conversations. These two also seemed to have fallen into place. Five years in Singapore, the conversations used to happen when both sought silence. While silence happened when they desperately wanted to talk. It soon sunk into Swadha's consciousness that a couple who knew when to talk and when to be quiet were the ones who had hit the peace-spot in their relationship. Swadha began to love the quiet breakfasts at home. She understood togetherness wasn't necessarily about chirping all the time. Just as we lock our homes while moving out because it gives us a psychological peace that our belongings are safe, sometimes the mere presence of someone gives our mind the same psychological comfort. That the relationship was safe even if words were not being exchanged all the time. Talking happened only when needed.

Ironically enough, after those silent moments during the day, there was more to talk about when they lay beside each other in bed at night, or when they sat for dinner at home or even during their morning tea in their high-rise balcony, looking out to the polluted Gurugram sky.

'We can't live here when we have kids. Just look at the quality of air,' he'd said coughing, after a week in Gurugram, while sipping his morning tea.

When we have kids . . . Swadha smiled to herself. That would be their next stepping stone as a couple. She always believed that life was all about living certain universal truth bombs. Everyone experienced them in different degrees and intensity. Sometimes, the explosion of the same truth bombs—be it birth, heartbreak, losing people you love, betrayal from close ones, marriage, parenthood, old age, death—happened in different ways. The effect of these truth bombs and the way one handled their explosion pretty much defined one's life. Swadha was happy that it was Haasil who spoke of kids for the first time between them. It told her, against all her latent insecure instincts, that she was his permanence.

'Maybe I'll have a talk with Nitin. Perhaps we can shift to Bengaluru or some other place later.'

Swadha had only nodded. She was already fantasizing about being impregnated by the love of her life. *How many girls get that lucky?* she wondered.

It was not only the conversations with Haasil that felt fresher, but Swadha started noticing Haasil progressively taking charge of certain gender roles between them. This, too, happened over the past three months. Though they had full-time maids, it was Haasil who prepared the morning tea. In Singapore, it used to be Swadha who asked what the food menu should be on a daily basis, but in recent months, it was Haasil who asked her about it. His active involvement in domesticity somewhere turned Swadha on. She felt it showcased his intention to help evolve their marriage in the healthiest manner possible. Love is so much about action. And action was all she saw Haasil engage in. For her. For them. The marriage that she thought was starting to derail in its early years itself was finally running superfast and super smooth. And the best part, without her having to sit at the steering wheel.

The sex, too, had suddenly gone unpredictable. To begin with, in Singapore, they were constantly all over each other. Then came a phase where they did it as a ritual. Bordering on pleasing the other so the other did not complain that they weren't having enough sex. Then there was a lull. The act of intimacy became a responsibility rather than a primitive response. Thus, it lacked zing. But again, since the last few months, Haasil abruptly used to knock when she was taking a shower. And get in. During their bland Netflix-watching nights, lying down beside her, he suddenly used to take her hand and place it on his groin. His hardness, for her, didn't take much time to make her wet and crave for an immediate carnal union. This sudden shift to a 'teen-phase romance' made her fall in love with him in a different way. And during this, Swadha realized that falling in love with your partner multiple times during a relationship ensures you live the relationship the way you ought to.

Unknown to Swadha, Haasil's sudden and overt involvement in their marriage, however, didn't come from a place of care alone but a place of guilt within him. Every minute, since the last three months, Haasil went overboard with Swadha in every aspect of their marriage because, in his mind, he kept wondering: *What if Swadha learnt about his secret dalliance with Palki?*

Chapter 3

From the time the WhatsApp message had come from Palki, Haasil felt an unprecedented restlessness within. The business award function was followed by a dinner with close people which went on till 2 a.m. Once they reached home, Swadha slept holding on to Haasil, the way she held the award trophy on stage hours back. She felt both were her achievements. By then, Haasil had seen Palki's WhatsApp message a hundred times. And had only replied once: *Coming to you at our usual time.* Everything in his body and soul, since the reply, was drawing him to her.

Early next morning, Haasil changed into his jogging tracksuit and left a sleeping Swadha with a peck on her cheek. Instead of driving to the joggers' park close to his place, he drove to another sector in Gurugram. He parked his car outside the gate, quickly climbed up the stairs and knocked on the door. It was one single house where the landlord had put the upper floor on rent. The door was opened by Palki. Seeing Haasil, she hugged him tight. As if she had been waiting for him all night. Responding to her embrace, Haasil wondered that, if destiny had taken her away, it was destiny, again, that had brought her to him.

On Palki's birthday, when by chance Haasil spotted her crossing the road and then followed her, he had a sinking feeling in his stomach. *Was it her? Or wasn't it? How it could be her?* He was further confused when she said her name was Akshita Jha. *How can it be?* he wondered. Out of decency, he had to leave her alone that day. But Haasil couldn't focus on work nor could he sleep that night. The moment had stretched itself and stayed with him mentally.

The next day he made sure he went to the same place, at the same time. In his heart he was hoping to get lucky again. He did see Palki again. Crossing the same road. At around the same time. Haasil didn't stop her. Instead, he followed her on foot to her office. A little asking around told him it wasn't an office as such but a photographer's studio. He stationed himself in the Starbucks opposite the studio.

Hours later, Haasil found himself taking the Delhi metro for the first time since he had flown in from Singapore. His eyes were on 'Akshita'. She had AirPods on. And seemed to be enjoying some music as her foot was constantly tapping. *Didn't she recognize me?* Haasil wondered. *Or is it that, like me, she doesn't remember much?* Half an hour later, Haasil was standing right outside the house in Gurugram where she was putting up. Before she went in, Haasil did excuse himself to ask her about a random, fictitious address that she had no idea about. She didn't seem to recognize him even from the day before. She couldn't possibly be pretending to not recognize me, he thought. Or was she was just a lookalike of Palki? Haasil's gut said it had to be the former. As he watched her enter the house, climb the stairs and lock herself in, Haasil couldn't help but lament at the irony of it all. Was it even real what was happening with him? He had suddenly spotted his ex-wife after seven years of her being presumed dead. All Haasil knew was he didn't have time to lose now. He couldn't go home and spend another sleepless night wondering about the plausibility of it all. Whatever it was—true or untrue—he had to figure it out right then and there.

Haasil took out his phone and searched for a particular picture. He spotted it after scrolling for some time in his gallery. The picture was of his tattoo. *Haasil-Palki* tattooed on him. He took a deep breath and went inside the house. A few unsure seconds later, he took the stairs to the floor above.

When Palki opened the door, she seemed surprised on seeing the stranger who had asked her about an address now at her doorstep.

'Is there any problem?' she asked. Haasil simply flashed his phone with the picture on display.

'Does this mean anything to you?' he said with bated breath. And saw Palki's expression change from curiosity to amazement to disbelief.

'I have the same tattoo with the name Palki first,' she said seeing the picture. At that moment, Haasil thought it surely was all unreal. He felt he was in a deep dream from which he would wake up at some point. He had already accepted the disappointment that would follow till he heard her ask, 'How do you have this picture?' And that's when Haasil realized this was actually real. The impossible had happened. Palki was alive. And he had discovered her quite unintentionally. The same universe that had worked to break them apart was working slyly to get them back again. She was the same one he had lost due to an accident. And life wasn't the same from there on. Neither for him nor for her. Haasil didn't know if he was smiling through his tears or crying through his smile.

'Is everything all right?' she asked.

'Yeah. I need to ask you something,' he said. She let him inside her house. Haasil looked around and sensed she was alone at the time.

'May I know where you were all these years?' Haasil asked.

As she spoke, Haasil learnt how Palki was first found by Hariharan, kept almost under an unsaid house arrest there for some years after which she finally escaped and went to work on a construction site. Till one day she was spotted by a photographer who not only clicked her but later invited her to come to Gurugram with him since the photos he had clicked of her had become a rage and he wanted her to pose for him. With the lure that she would get to be in the city, she gave in. When he learnt she had no memory of her past, he helped her begin anew by naming her Akshita Jha. She did try to trace her past but reached a cul-de-sac. The photographer told her that he did publish her photographs in some newspapers—under the 'Missing' section—but got no response. She accepted herself as Akshita and began a new life ever since she became his model. It was the photographer who had helped her put up here. By the time she was done, Haasil could feel his heart racing. He couldn't help but admire the way life's screenplay worked.

'What's your story?' she asked.

It was Haasil's turn to tell her all that he underwent after the accident. That he too had amnesia but his condition wasn't as hopeless as Palki's. He had only lost his recent memory, not his entire life like her. He skipped the Pallavi part for he didn't know how Palki would react. And it was not important for him. What was important was finally, against all hopes, he had found Palki. The only love of his life. Palki was stunned on hearing Haasil. She always knew the name, read it on her tattoo as well, sometimes even murmured it under her breath but only now she knew the story she had forgotten. When an awkward silence crept up after they both were done narrating the past, Haasil realized there was one thing life had gotten totally wrong. The timing of Palki's reappearance.

Though Haasil didn't want to leave, he had to. At home, for the first time in years, he couldn't look Swadha in the eye. There was a constant storm within him asking, *What now?* Haasil wasn't ready for this twist in his life. Not now. Had it happened before he had married Swadha, everything would have fallen into place. Now everything seemed wrong. One small step and he was running the risk of becoming the villain in Swadha's life as much as he would be the hero in Palki's.

The next day onwards, Haasil started meeting Palki every day. He brought all the photographs he had of her. Of them. Their past. Their love story. It was all vague for Palki but, caressing those photographs, she understood what an ugly turn life had taken for them through the accident. Every day, Haasil came to her with some story or the other that Nitin had told him years ago when he was recuperating from the accident. He informed her about the untimely demise of her parents. He did propose to Palki that he could take her to meet her relatives, but Palki herself didn't want that. The irony of the situation, Haasil realized, was that he was doing the same thing to Palki that Nitin had done to him once Haasil had opened his eyes after the accident. Retriggering her memories with information. Haasil could empathize with Palki in the process. It was the same frustration, of trying to grasp one own's life, she was going through that he himself had experienced once.

At home, whenever Swadha was there, Haasil felt guilty of hiding things from her. She had absolutely no idea of what was going on in his life. They were life partners. She had the right to know about the big discovery that Haasil had encountered in the form of Palki. But how could he tell her? His discovery of Palki was in direct contrast to Swadha's role in his life. What would he tell her? That he went to meet Palki every morning, telling Swadha that he was going for a morning jog? Even though there was nothing sexual between Palki and him yet, emotionally, Haasil had started to belong to Palki more than Swadha from the moment she reappeared in his life. And to compensate for this feeling of his, Haasil's actions at home became more Swadha-centric. The excess bit, which he had once accused Swadha of, now became his habit towards her. His unsaid, but deeply felt, redemption. Every time there was a pang of guilt accusing him of betrayal, Haasil would immediately plan a surprise dinner for Swadha, or buy her a costly gift or simply make wild and wicked love to her. His wrong didn't only lie in the fact that he allowed himself to cross the line of fidelity or hide the presence of Palki in his life from Swadha, but it was that he never let himself introspect about the situation. He simply kept repeating the same wrong on a daily basis. The first day when he had met Palki it was done unknowingly, but the next day onwards it was all an intentional sin.

On the other hand, Haasil did take Palki to a psychologist, even a psychoanalyst and to neurologists as well for check-ups to know if everything was all right with her medically. Since, as per Palki's account, no doctor had ever checked her after the accident. Thankfully, she was fine.

In the next three months, Haasil had apologized to Palki several times, saying he should have waited for her. But he understood how complex a human being could be when Palki asked him, 'Do you have anyone in your life?' And he found himself saying, 'No, I'm single.' Haasil always believed in monogamy but, in one moment, he had contradicted himself. And when she asked him to take her to his place, he further surprised himself with cunning excuses to avoid doing so. Was he always a liar, a manipulator or was it just the situation? Haasil couldn't put a finger on one aspect. He hated himself and yet he couldn't stop being what he hated himself for.

And at present, as they broke their embrace standing right at Palki's doorstep, Haasil kissed her forehead and said, 'I still can't believe I've found you. It's all a chance, I know, but . . .' Palki kissed his forehead and thought, *We didn't meet by chance, honey. My intention is simple. I want to finish you, Haasil Sinha.*

Chapter 4

It was ladies' night out. Swadha and Sanjana were sipping their favourite poison sitting amidst the foot-thumping music in one of Gurugram's most happening nightclubs.

'You want to step out for a smoke?' Sanjana asked.

'Since when did you start smoking?' Swadha asked and followed her out. It was only when Swadha had moved to Gurugram from Singapore that she started getting to know Sanjana as a person. Before that, she was just the hubby's bestie's girl. In Gurugram, they used to visit the salon and go shopping together. The intensity with which consuming alcohol together connected men, shopping together did the same to women. And that was not all. They took their Pilates and lawn tennis classes together as well. The more time Swadha spent with Sanjana, the more she realized how carefree a woman Sanjana was. She was a quick decision-maker, who never let any problem get big on her and always knew how to smile through the shitty things of life. There was much to learn from her, Swadha understood.

Standing outside the nightclub, Sanjana took out a box which looked brand new. She pulled out a cigarette from it and offered one to Swadha. She politely declined. Sanjana lighted hers. Took a nervous drag.

'I smoke only when I'm stressed,' Sanjana said. Swadha was glad her question hadn't fallen on deaf ears. But the answer naturally led to another question.

'What's stressing you?' Swadha asked. This was the first time Swadha had heard her use the word 'stress'.

'I missed my periods,' Sanjana said abruptly.

'Oh!' Swadha understood what she meant. 'But what's the stress about?'

Sanjana looked at her. Swadha noticed she was moist-eyed.

'I don't want to be a mother.'

How does one respond to something like that? Swadha wondered. And saw Sanjana throw a sharp glance at her.

'Judging me?' she asked.

'Of course not. It's your body. You get to decide what you want, when you want.'

'I know. But I also know I would be termed as less of a woman by Nitin's family. And probably him as well. I don't know about the rest of the world but a woman in India can't say no to motherhood. It's a given. If she is a woman, she needs to be a mother sooner or later.'

There was silence as Swadha felt a few more ladies, standing some distance away and busy smoking, were eyeing them casually. Sanjana definitely stated a fact. The right to motherhood, ironically enough, was rarely about the mother's choice in the culture she, too, was brought up in. But to shrug off the most basic demand, or gift, of nature from you was sure surprising for her. She wanted to ask Sanjana a lot but didn't know if it was the right time. Sanjana dabbed her cigarette out in one of the common ashtrays and then lit another one.

'Tell me, Swadha, is it really important to sync your desires to a societal timeline?'

'It's not important but, to be honest, it's damn difficult to sever yourself from it. Everyone's conditioned to be so deep within it. I mean, the first ones to judge you would be the women more than the men.'

The way Sanjana locked her eyes with Swadha's told the latter she had understood the subtext.

Sanjana didn't speak after that. Swadha waited till she finished her second cigarette. Then they went inside and finished their drinks quietly, after which Swadha called for the bill.

In the next fifteen minutes they were in the parking lot.

'Did you talk to Nitin?' Swadha asked. They stood in-between their parked cars.

Sanjana sounded stoic when she spoke, 'Just squeezed in the motherhood part.'

'What did he say?'

'I didn't tell him that I never wanted to be a mother. I've realized in marriage you need to let your partner sip rather than gulp information like this. I just told him I want to focus on work now. In fact, that's why I took my time to get married even though I knew Nitin was the one. Till then, I was convinced that he understood where I was coming from. That's why you invest time and life with someone, right? So they know you well enough along with the places you belong to within yourself, so the questions wear off over time.' Sanjana looked around, contemplating her words.

'But,' she continued, 'these days he suddenly seems to have changed. Now he tells me all the time that it's just my mind. That women are hardwired to handle family and work together. But I know myself.'

'Does Nitin know you missed your periods?'

'I'm pregnant, Swadha. There were two lines on the test kit this morning. I haven't told Nitin because I know what he is going to say.'

Swadha shrugged.

Sanjana went on, 'The same bloody thing. You will be able to do it. And when I won't, I know I'll have to choose family over work. That's what women are supposed to prefer, right? That's how my mother also ended up giving up her desires after having me. For a woman, society chooses what her first priority should be. She is only allowed to choose whatever comes second and third for herself.'

There was a haunting silence.

'Now that you've tested, you have to inform Nitin, right?' Swadha asked. Sanjana gave her a prolonged look and told her about what she had in mind.

The next week, Swadha accompanied Sanjana to a gynaecologist where they ended up aborting the foetus. Sanjana couldn't thank Swadha enough for the emotional support. But staying with Sanjana through the abortion, Swadha's own motherly instincts were triggered. She started wondering whether Haasil and she should start talking about having a family. Haasil was particular about having protected sex, more so in the last few months. It clearly showed he didn't even want to take a chance. But what's the harm, she argued within. They had a good life, good careers and all the other social ticks were done. The next obvious step was to have a family of their own. And, unlike Sanjana, Swadha wanted to be a mother sometime.

During the weekend, when both were watching Netflix, cosying up in bed, Swadha did whisper it into Haasil's ears.

'Do you think we should have a family now?'

Haasil neither looked surprised nor did he come up with a casual yes or no. Instead, he looked flustered. She sensed a simmering irritation in him. As if Swadha had mentioned something blasphemous. She couldn't fathom why, because she didn't know that her motherhood would be a deterrent in Haasil–Palki's renewed love story. And Haasil wasn't ready for that.

Chapter 5

Pallavi was waiting impatiently for Eerav in a bistro in Bengaluru. The last time they had met was a month back, in Delhi itself, at Pallavi's place. Eerav had come all excited after ghosting yet another married woman. That way, Pallavi and Eerav were twin flames of sorts. Though to begin with, Eerav wasn't as smooth with his approach as Pallavi was with men, but since they started being each other's human diary, Eerav took all of Pallavi's confessions as a learning toolkit and applied them to the women he dated. The results of which gave him a greater high than the encounters themselves.

Eerav knew about Haasil from Pallavi. He learnt about Palki only after Pallavi saw the photograph at the exhibition. Though Pallavi wasn't an exact lookalike, Eerav noticed, after comparing her with the profile photograph of Palki that his friend had clicked, certain portions seemed like an exact replica. A trick of nature, Eerav concluded, since the two ladies had different gene pools but one common point in their destinies—Haasil. But what Pallavi had told him after she had brought Palki to Delhi and stationed her at a rented place, was something Eerav wasn't ready for. They were ghosting people for fun and some twisted personal healing, but Pallavi's plan for Haasil and Palki was pure evil. Not that he mentioned his opinion to her. It was their cardinal rule. The other couldn't suggest or opine about the other's confession. Unless asked for. And Pallavi had not asked for his advice on the matter. She was conclusive about her plan.

While waiting for him in the bistro, Pallavi was busy checking out the pictures that Palki had messaged her. And they weren't pictures of Palki alone. They were private, intimate selfies that Palki had clicked with Haasil. In cafés, in cinema halls, in the mall, in salons, in nightclubs. Nothing too intimate but anyone seeing the pictures would know they were dating. Proof was important, Pallavi thought, in the grand scheme of things that she had thought out in her mind. And it all started the day she saw Palki's photograph at the exhibition.

A curiosity-wind blew within her the moment her eyes fell on the photograph. Her gut knew who could it be. But her mind asked her to be sure first. In police records, Pallavi did a quick calculation, it was the seventh year of Palki's going missing. She would be presumed dead soon. Or maybe she already was, since Pallavi didn't remember the month of the accident. When Eerav's friend Mahesh Solanki, whose exhibition it was and who was a kind of celebrity in the photography circuit, came and expressed his amazement at the facial similarity, Pallavi immediately inquired where had he met the woman in the photograph. Mahesh gave her the exact location. It was after the exhibition, when she was drinking at a pub with Eerav, that Pallavi told him she was going to find the woman in the photograph. She'd never sounded as excited as she did while speaking of Palki, Eerav had noted. As if Pallavi had reconnected with her soul after a long time. The excitement wasn't about finding Palki but the numerous possibilities it contained for her to get back at Haasil. Get back at the man who single-handedly had performed a failed surgery on her inside, the after-effects of which she was taking to her grave.

She had asked Mahesh if he had spoken to the woman in the photograph. He said he did but very little and too casual. According to him, the woman asked him all sorts of questions. She was fluent in English and Hindi. It didn't surprise Mahesh for he had guessed the lady was the odd one out amongst the locals. That was one reason why he'd spotted her in the first place. She wanted to come to the city with him. He had asked her to wait right there so he could finish his photography but when he came there after a few hours, she was gone. Unlike what Palki had told Haasil about her coming to the city, as per Pallavi's direction, the truth was something else. The only solid information Pallavi got from Mahesh was the woman's location. Pallavi, a few days after the exhibition, reached the place alone.

Once there, it struck her—whom should she ask for? The language barrier was one thing. The second, which she realized only after reaching the place, was that nobody knew Palki by her name. Either she had a different name or she didn't remember it herself. And she didn't have any photograph of hers either. She hoped, perhaps, that their facial similarity would lead Pallavi to her via people who had seen Palki.

Pallavi started showing the locals around her own photograph from her phone with the profile that matched Palki the most. The ones who looked at the photograph stared at her. It was obvious. They thought she was showing them her own photograph. And wondered if she had lost her mind. It was only after three hours of relentless searching and asking almost everyone in the small hamlet that Pallavi decided to return without a clue as to where Palki was. She assumed that perhaps Palki had moved on from the place. The fact that she had not contacted Haasil yet and was still living somewhere in an unknown hamlet made her conclude Palki most definitely didn't have her past memory either. Just like the accident had affected Haasil with retrograde amnesia.

Exhausted, Pallavi decided to get into her car and go back. She was dejected as never before. It was while she was drinking some water inside the car, when the driver she had hired to get her here, turned to her and said, 'Madam, if you don't mind, I think you are trying to find someone.'

Pallavi nodded, finishing the water from her bottle.

'My relatives work at a construction site nearby. You want to check there?'

'How far is it?' she asked.

'Thirty minutes from here.'

Pallavi thought for a few seconds. She wasn't going to return here again for sure. Thirty minutes wouldn't make the trip any worse. She nodded at the driver.

It took her that much time to reach the construction site. As the driver parked the car outside, he again turned to say, 'If you don't want to get down, madam, I can ask around.' By then, he had understood the sun was taxing Pallavi. She gave him the phone with her photograph and sat back in the car.

Though the driver gave her a furtive glance on seeing the photograph, he didn't inquire about anything else. Except for saying in an excited tone, 'Oh, it's a real case of lookalikes, madam. We have this a lot in our films.'

He stepped out and disappeared from sight. A few minutes later, he came running back and told Pallavi that the security guard at the site told him someone who looked similar was staying and working at the site. Pallavi literally jumped out of the car hearing him.

She felt a knot in her stomach on seeing Palki. The obvious similarity in their looks was not very pronounced thanks to Palki's near-shabby looks, long hair and unwaxed lip line. This was the first time she was seeing her this close. The last time was when she'd seen her with Haasil when they were teens. Palki looked confused. And curious. For the first time in years, someone had reached her. Asked for her. She was sure the person knew her. The irony was, Palki didn't know her.

'I'm sorry but I don't know you,' Palki said in her soft voice.

'I know. Don't worry, I'll take you back to the world which the accident made you leave,' Pallavi said and noticed a faint smile on Palki's face. *She knows about the accident too*, Palki thought. Though she herself didn't remember the accident, Palki had guessed from her wounds years ago that something bad had happened to her.

'Why didn't you wait for the photographer?' Pallavi asked once they were in the car.

'I did.' Palki understood whom she was referring to. 'But he never turned up and I had to come here.'

Pallavi understood it was a case of mistiming. It was during their four-hour long drive to Bengaluru that Pallavi had decided on her plan. A plan that would destroy the one who had destroyed her from within. And didn't let her experience life the way she would have had he not happened to her.

'What's that smirk about? Another dick pic?' said Eerav, who had joined her at the bistro. He had caught her smiling at a picture of Palki and Haasil in the former's balcony which had made her reminisce about her meeting with Palki. Pallavi closed the picture the moment she saw Eerav. They embraced tightly. He glanced at her.

'What happened?' he asked.

'What, what happened?'

'You look . . .'

'Happy?'

'Exactly.'

'You're surprised seeing me happy. That tells me what a shitty sob life I must have been living.'

They settled down.

'I thought you already knew that yourself.' Eerav sat down opposite her. 'But I do sense something unprecedented has happened. Your vibe is a little different tonight.'

'Is it?'

'Yeah,' he nodded, 'Can't put a finger on it still,' he said, looking at Pallavi's drink.

'Absolut,' she said. Eerav ordered one for him.

'So, what's happening?' he asked.

'Maybe the vibe changed because finally I see some moksha for myself,' Pallavi said, sipping her drink.

'Is that what good sex does to people these days? Leads them to moksha?' Eerav braced himself to listen to her new sexual escapade. But what he heard next took him by surprise.

'Haasil thinks Palki actually wants him back in her life. And he lied to her about him being single. This is what is called soul-revenge. Years ago, he had unintentionally revealed the bitch in me. Now, I have revealed the demon in him.' Pallavi burst into prolonged laughter.

Seeing a diabolical gleam in her eyes as she laughed, Eerav judged her for the first time since they had met. He felt tempted to tell her to back off for his gut told him that whatever she had in mind would take her to a point of no return.

Eerav's gut feeling was correct.

Chapter 6

'It's not that, Swadha,' Haasil said on the video call. Swadha was at a spa. She lay on her tummy, only her buttocks were covered with a towel, while her head was placed on a soft, wet cloth ring and her mouth was hanging open downward from a hole in the bed for easy breathing. A young girl was massaging her back. Swadha could hear Haasil loud and clear through her AirPods while she could see him on her mobile screen kept on the floor right below her eyes. It was the umpteenth time they were discussing 'family'.

It started during the celebratory dinner after the business award show. Everyone was happy for Swadha. She could sense a restlessness in Haasil but she couldn't guess why. Her attention was drawn towards her family discussing how she had achieved everything and perhaps it was time she gave ear to her mother's instinct. Though she respected Sanjana's perspective, personally she felt the crowning achievement of every woman was about being a mother.

Realizing Haasil wouldn't agree with her, Swadha ended the call and decided to revel in the massage for the time being.

Sanjana's abortion onwards, every time Swadha tried to discuss family with Haasil, he feigned some excuse or the other. Then one night she asked him to his face, 'If you don't want a baby, tell me straight. Getting ignored all the time is insulting.'

Haasil understood he had to talk to her right then. He took her to the high-rise deck, made her sit on the swing and after taking in some air, said, 'I'm not trying to discourage you, but I shall state some facts. It's not that we are ageing. We both are still in the pink of health to produce kids any time we want. But what is more important right now is our business. We both have given our sweat to it. And I can't pull it through alone.' Haasil knew he was bullshitting. But he had to. Deep within he knew he could still handle Swadha and Palki. But he couldn't manage Swadha, Palki and a baby.

'It's not that I will be pinned to the bed all the time. I will be there with you, baby,' Swadha tried to argue. The argument kept shuttling like a tennis ball from one court to the other till Swadha said, 'Okay, whatever!'

After the spa, she brought it up a few more times but every time, Haasil had some excuse or the other. The entire ordeal of convincing him was tiring Swadha emotionally. She understood he wasn't ready, perhaps. She did some online reading after doing a Google search and understood certain men have apprehensions about getting into the father mode. It is to do with their settling-down instinct. She chose to give him a few more months.

'All right. But by the end of this year, I won't listen to you any more,' Swadha said conclusively, turning the other way on the bed and going to sleep. Haasil was awake, though.

He realized time was running out. And he had to take a decision. He had lied to Palki about his marital status, while Swadha didn't know about Palki's re-emergence in his life. This couldn't be a permanent arrangement. Nor was having a baby with Swadha. In fact, it would make him more answerable to his marriage with Swadha. He didn't sleep that night. But by the time it was dawn, Haasil had made a choice. He would choose Palki over Swadha.

Haasil intentionally dropped his caring attitude towards Swadha. He wanted to be so difficult with her that it would give her the feeling that the marriage wasn't working any more. That it was a plain and simple mistake. And the calling-off would then come from Swadha herself. Not that Haasil was happy doing this. He justified his changed behaviour in his mind, saying it was life that had created such a situation for him and he no longer had an option that would not harm anyone. If he chose Swadha, Palki and he both would be hurt. If he chose Palki, Swadha would be hurt. Choosing Palki was more correct for him because he was actually in love with her. With Swadha, it was more of an emotional arrangement he had brought himself to make for his own selfish reasons.

Haasil's changed behaviour wasn't limited to home alone. Even in the office he started being more and more distant. Swadha had no clue why it was all happening. One silly fight led to more serious fights. He started showing his irritation in almost everything she did. As if he had a problem with everything she did, said or thought.

It was only when Haasil was with Palki that he remained at peace with himself. Her presence was balm to his inner chaos. It told him that to get something right, one has to do some wrong somewhere. Till one day Palki asked him something that he knew would come up but didn't expect it would happen so soon.

'Let's get married again, Haasil,' she said while they were having dinner at her place. After a long time, she had cooked for him. He felt her hands grasping his when she said it. He was at her place for five straight hours. A first of sorts for them. All of Swadha's calls and messages had been ignored.

Haasil didn't respond immediately even though their eyes were locked. When he did, he couldn't lie this time.

'I'm already married, Palki.' He hadn't felt so embarrassed as he did at that moment. If there was one person who perhaps deserved the truth from him, it was Palki. Lying to her in the first place was a mistake; Haasil had understood it by then. He couldn't lie to her a second time.

Haasil felt Palki swiftly withdraw her hands from his. There was an awkward silence as they were in between their meal. In the immediate minute following, the silence turned probing. Haasil felt it would engulf him whole. Then he saw her get up without finishing her meal. She said, 'I think it's late. You should leave.' Her voice was heavy. But her mind was overjoyed. She couldn't wait to update Pallavi about this.

Chapter 7

I t took Haasil by surprise when Nitin, over a drink post office hours, asked if everything was all right between Swadha and him.

'Yeah, all's well. Why do you ask?' Haasil said, sensing Nitin was in two minds about what he wanted to say. When he heard Nitin, Haasil was all the more furious. Why would Swadha share something that was between a husband and wife with his friend? Even if he was his best friend.

'I think you guys should visit a gynaecologist once. I guess that's what Swadha also wants,' Nitin said. It took two quick pegs for Haasil to calm his sudden anger down. Haasil stayed quiet because he didn't want to say anything in the moment that could affect his relationship with Nitin again. This time it wasn't even his fault.

When Haasil was on his fourth drink, he felt an impulse to tell Nitin that he had found Palki. That he was ready to forget everything that had happened after the accident till now. That he wanted to live a life with her, not Swadha. Swadha wasn't a mistake but was mistiming. He remained quiet. Instead, before they went home, Haasil agreed to fulfil Nitin's request justifying that he wasn't getting time for the gynaecologist visit. He didn't want Nitin to get a sniff of his personal reality.

On reaching home, Haasil had a massive fight with Swadha.

'Will Nitin decide whether I should go to a gynae or not?' he said.

'Nitin isn't deciding. He just requested you to do so on my behalf,' Swadha said. Having seen Haasil lose his cool at the drop of a hat of late, this avatar didn't surprise her any more. 'And you know why he did that, Haasil? Because you have stopped listening to me.'

Swadha's high pitch didn't infuriate him as much as the disturbing truth in her words did. It made Haasil walk out of the room. The truth was that this fight, and the countless other fights they had already had by then, was his doing. He had literally manufactured them to squeeze out a decision about their marriage from Swadha.

Sitting in his study, he called Palki. She didn't pick up. He left a message. And scrolled through their WhatsApp chat. Palki had not replied nor seen his messages since two days now. He knew why. Now he felt he shouldn't have told her the truth. But where was the lie leading them? Nowhere. He decided to give Palki some time.

When he woke up in the morning, Haasil noticed a cup of coffee on the centre table. He had slept on the couch itself. He sighed, got up and looked at the coffee mug. It had a picture of Swadha and him on it. They both looked happy. Haasil picked up the mug. He ambled to the balcony where Swadha was already sipping her coffee, sitting on the swing.

Haasil came up and touched his mug to her exposed arm. She squirmed, acknowledging his presence.

'Haasil, please, I'm not in the mood,' she said.

'Let me know when you want me to go to the gynae,' Haasil said, sipping his coffee. Swadha gave him an exasperated look.

'Are you serious?' she asked. Haasil nodded and added, 'I'm sorry for last night.'

Swadha got up and hugged him tight.

A week later, they were sitting in front of one of the leading gynaecologists in New Delhi. She had listed some basic tests for both and after a preliminary check-up, told them everything seemed fine outwardly. They were asked to come back with their reports.

One set of the tests were for Haasil. He was supposed to give his semen sample for examination. He did as asked but not at the in-house facility of the clinic. He chose to do it from a separate diagnostic centre. Swadha didn't find it important enough to make an issue of it. When the report arrived in his email inbox, he read the PDF immediately. Everything read all right with him. Same for Swadha. Haasil downloaded the PDF, converted it into a .doc file and altered the report, showing everything was wrong with him. Then he converted it into a PDF and WhatsApped it to Swadha. It was his way of postponing what Swadha was hell-bound to experience.

Haasil was prescribed multivitamins along with some more tests, but every time the doctor saw the report that Haasil brought with him, she couldn't help but be shocked. Be it his sperm count or his DNA fragmentation or his sperm motility, everything seemed to have been affected.

'I think we should give it a break,' Haasil said, when they were driving to the office together.

'Didn't get you.'

'All this medical shit. It's getting to me now.'

Swadha sympathized with him for she understood it wasn't easy. Getting tested every time with a hope, only to be told you aren't ready yet for natural conception, was heartbreaking for Swadha. And she hoped the same was the case for Haasil as well.

'Let's just wait for few more months and then try? The doctor said a healthy diet and lifestyle should lead to better results along with the medicines,' Haasil proposed.

'Yeah, I think so too.'

After a long time, they seemed to have agreed on something. That itself made Swadha happy. There was nothing for her to doubt that Haasil was sabotaging the medical reports. With Swadha agreeing to give it some time, Haasil made up his mind that this was the time when he would have to instil a separation trigger from her. It was now or never.

Moving out of the office that day, citing a business lunch, Haasil drove straight to Palki's place. It had been close to a month that they had physically met since he had told her he wasn't single. Palki did respond to messages and also had a phone conversation with him, but every time he wanted to meet, she avoided the matter. But Palki's voice told him how morose she had become since he had confessed the truth about his relationship status. As if something had sucked the life out of her. Haasil, in particular, felt her hurt when she told him that he would never understand what it felt like to have someone else snatch her life away. Swadha, according to Palki, was living her life. She was enjoying that which Palki was entitled to. And she couldn't come to terms with that. Haasil didn't blame her either. If he had been in Palki's place, he too wouldn't have been calm seeing her married to someone else, presuming he was dead. He thought hard for days. Then decided to meet Palki and include her in his plan of divorcing Swadha. That way, at least one of the ladies would live in peace. And so would he.

Haasil parked his Maybach outside the house. Stepped out and swiftly took the staircase up. The landlord stopped him in between, calling out from below. Haasil turned and came down.

'She left the place this morning,' the landlord said. 'The house is locked now.'

It was a gut-punch for Haasil. A strange fear gripped him instantly. He couldn't lose Palki again. The last time he had somehow survived. Now he wouldn't, Haasil was sure. He most certainly wouldn't.

As Haasil turned to leave, the landlord stopped him again.

'She left this note,' he said, holding out a piece of paper. Haasil took it, and unfolded it to read the message written there: *I'M SORRY, HAASIL*.

Haasil could only think of the worst.

Chapter 8

Leaving the house and getting into his Maybach, Haasil called Palki ten times on the trot. He did hear the ring each time on the other end but nobody picked up. He left messages on WhatsApp and waited for half an hour, sitting tight in his car with the AC on full blast, keeping the phone's screen open and hoping she would come on WhatsApp. His thumb was on the WhatsApp call button, ready to call if Palki came online. She didn't. Not in the half hour that Haasil had stayed put in his car. Nor were his messages read throughout the day.

Haasil decided to go to the photo studio where she worked as a model but he was told Palki was on indefinite leave. Did he lose her again? This time forever? Unlike before, this time she had gone of her own free will. The last thought made him all the more anxious. It didn't allow Haasil to be in peace. He felt responsible for breaking her heart with his lie. If he had told her the truth—that he was married—at the very beginning and explained how and why it had happened, the damage wouldn't have been this much. He was guilty of leading her to believe, through the lie, that there were possibilities between them and convincing her that the accident had not taken anything away from their love story. It had. It had taken the most precious of elements of a love story: time. And they were paying the price, for time is never constant. It was in their favour before the accident. Then it decided to turn its back on them. And now it was flashing its dry sense of humour.

Haasil didn't know what to do next. Should he go to the police? Share everything with Nitin? Confess to Swadha? En route to the office, Haasil kept thinking about it all. His worries escalated when he realized that none of these were viable options for him. It would further complicate things with Palki going off the radar. He decided to wait for a few days. Just to give her that time to be at peace with herself, their situation and then probably she would get in touch again. It was hope against hope, he knew.

Swadha was used to Haasil's aloofness. So much so that she had taken it as his normal state. She didn't feel like fighting it any more. A point comes in a relationship where you know you can't leave the relationship but you also feel it's okay to put it on autopilot mode and just go wherever it takes you. Swadha found herself in that state of mind. The balance of silence and conversation between them had shifted. Now she chose deliberate silences where she knew talking was necessary.

A few nights later, when Haasil retired to bed, turned away from her and was seemingly asleep, Swadha put her hand on him. It had been months since they had made love. For some time she wanted him to initiate it, then she understood he wouldn't and was okay with it. Now she decided to test if sexual intimacy could break the emotional ice that had formed between them. What happened next made Swadha see a different Haasil. Someone she wasn't in love with.

Haasil reacted to her touch by turning his head to her. Before she realized it, he was kissing her. A little aggressively. Then he did something that he had never done before. He bit her. On the lips to begin with, then the arms and thighs. They weren't soft bites. It seemed he was digging his canines into her skin as a mark of some revenge. Swadha shrieked out in pain. Asked him to stop. But Haasil didn't. Usually there was always a synergy in their stripping but this night was different. Haasil literally forced her nightdress and undies off. Got naked and turned her in the doggy position. A painful moan escaped her when he entered her. It was a hard thrust, not a gentle push to get in.

As he kept thrusting, full and hard, holding her hair and pulling it back, Swadha howled in pain, trying her best to get out of the act. She couldn't free herself from Haasil's strong hold. And then he started hurling abuses in her ear, softly at first. Then loudly. Lurid abuses that she hadn't heard him say to even a stranger on the road. *Who was this man? She couldn't possibly love this guy. Why was she with him?* Swadha wondered in tears. The relentless spanking didn't come from a place of intimacy, kinkiness or love. He was giving her pain—raw pain—she realized.

Once he was done, Haasil pushed her on the bed as if she wasn't his wife but a piece of filth he had picked up from the street, used and abused, and now that he was done, had to dispose of her. Swadha had never felt so humiliated before. When Haasil left the room, she was in shock. So much so that not a word nor even a cry came out of her. She thought she had lost her voice. The pain didn't let her get up. Sleep was a far cry that night.

In the morning, Haasil entered the bedroom with an apologetic face. He did recollect last night's incident, and lay in the hall for the remainder of the night until morning. He couldn't believe what he had done. Something for which he knew there could be no apology. He was angry, frustrated, loathsome towards life, already flustered because of Palki, when he had retired to bed. In his mind, he was going through the shit storm that had hit them both. He was desperately desirous of one tangible human form on whom he could rest all his blame and accusations. Swadha became that human. The anger, the frustration, the abhorrence towards life and the situation he was in were all directed towards Swadha. He wasn't making love to her, he was punishing her for being in love with him.

'I'm deeply sorry,' Haasil said, approaching a hurt-looking Swadha, curled up in bed. It was pretty evident she hadn't slept either.

'This won't ever happen again. I mean it. And just because I'm saying this won't happen again, you don't have to forgive me. I shall take whatever you decide. I deserve every bit of shit you throw at me.'

With tears rolling down her cheeks, Swadha said, 'You made me question the image of the man I have been in love with, married to, Haasil. I'll never forgive you for that.' She stood up and went to the washroom, closing the door with a loud thud. The sound wasn't of the wood alone, but the extent of her hurt as well.

Sitting pensively in his office cabin later in the day, Haasil could see Swadha through the glass wall, working in her cabin. Though her dress covered the places where he had bitten her, Haasil knew the wounds would not have healed. When he had gone to her in the morning to apologize, he noticed her skin had turned purple wherever he had bitten her. He didn't have the guts to say anything about her bruises then.

Not once did Swadha glance at him. It was unlike her. Fighting with Swadha so she pulled out of the marriage was one thing, but becoming an abusive man was something he himself had zero tolerance for. Sitting wrapped in silence, Haasil checked his WhatsApp again. There was still nothing from Palki. *Was there nothing he could do?* he wondered.

Post lunch, Haasil headed to the photo studio. He introduced himself and asked the lady who received him there to connect him to the owner. An hour later, Mahesh came in. Haasil first explained his connection to Palki and requested Mahesh to connect him to Palki. Seeing Haasil's vulnerability and understanding the gravity of the situation, Mahesh called Palki. She picked up. Mahesh asked her about her whereabouts. Cross-checked what Haasil had told him to know if he was genuine.

'When are you coming back? A lot of photo shoots are pending,' Mahesh said.

'I'm not keeping mentally well. But I will be back in a week's time. Really sorry about this, Mahesh,' Palki said. She sounded morose.

'I also heard you have shifted. Any problem?'

As Palki spoke, Mahesh was able to squeeze out her present address. Haasil rushed there and reached after fifteen minutes of driving.

Palki rolled her eyes seeing Haasil at the door.

'Oh Mahesh, why?' she feigned, looking exasperated.

She left the door open and went in to sit on the couch. Haasil stepped in. One look around, he realized it was a better furnished place than the last one.

'I hope you understand, Palki, eluding me won't help either you or me.'

'Really? Then what am I supposed to do? Be happy with the fact that you're married? And you chose not to tell me about it before?' Palki sounded cross.

Haasil came up to her, knelt down to be in her line of sight and said, 'I'm sorry I lied. But I didn't do it to scam you in any way. I did it because I didn't want to lose you.'

Palki was listening intently. Haasil went on for a few minutes.

'. . . And I promise, Swadha and I will be divorcing soon.'

Palki spoke after a thoughtful pause.

'I need some space. I don't know what to feel or say right now.'

'Sure. Take your time. But just don't leave me like this.'

Palki nodded. Some silent minutes later, Haasil left. It was then Pallavi appeared from the other room.

The way the two ladies smiled at each other, it was clear. In the plan to destroy Haasil, they were in it . . . together.

Chapter 9

When Pallavi picked up Palki from the construction site near Bengaluru, she had initially thought of flying Palki to New Delhi with her, but during her drive to the city, Pallavi understood her assumptions were right. That Palki didn't have much memory of her previous life. Unlike Haasil, she had lost those memories that were long nested. It meant the past had been erased. The only thing she remembered were vague moments hovering around the accident. By the time Pallavi reached Bengaluru, she had decided she would drive Palki to New Delhi.

It took them numerous stops and three days of driving to reach her place. During the journey, Pallavi did talk to Palki but sparsely. She was mostly observing her. The similarity of their faces did amaze Palki as well but it was more in her expressions than in her words. Once at Pallavi's flat, Palki had a good shower, after which she sat opposite Pallavi in the deck area overlooking the Gurugram skyline, with some steaming black coffee and an English breakfast prepared by Pallavi placed between them on a table.

'We aren't blood-related,' Pallavi chose to clarify the first and obvious thing. 'We look a little similar but that's just nature running out of its own permutations and combinations, perhaps.'

'Then how do you know me?'

'It's a long story but I won't cut it short. If you don't know it then you won't know the one who is responsible for your condition. The one who caused the accident.' Pallavi was careful about the words she chose. For the story she was about to sell to Palki, a lot depended on how she projected Haasil. Her entire plan of destroying him depended on how convinced Palki was with the story.

Palki frowned and then heard Pallavi say, 'It's a man behind it all. Haasil Sinha. The villain of your life.'

Pallavi's plan was to feed Palki with a false story, projecting Haasil as someone who had caused her downfall. She wanted to rile Palki up so much that she would take it on herself to pay Haasil back. This way she would not only destroy Haasil but also the root cause of all her bloody wounds and scars: the Haasil-Palki love story.

Pallavi didn't tell her everything immediately, though. Discovering Palki by chance at the photo exhibition wasn't just serendipity. It was the universe giving her an opportunity to heal herself by wounding the one who had wounded her. And for that she had to do her homework right. Everything depended on that.

'I'll tell you all of it but I need to fly in a few hours, so I need to get ready. I'm an air hostess by profession. I've ordered all the groceries. Stay here and take it easy. I shall be back in a couple of days. It's such a relief meeting you, Palki.'

Hearing her own name for the first time with such conviction from someone, Palki thought perhaps finally she would get her old life back. She was wrong.

Instead of two days, Pallavi returned almost two weeks later. Though she was in touch with Palki over the phone throughout that time. After dinner that night, Pallavi went inside and brought her laptop out. As she opened it, she started narrating her story.

'Now listen up. You are Palki Sinha, wife of Haasil Sinha. He runs a consulting firm along with his best friend and business partner, Nitin Punjabi.' She opened a website—NH Consultants—and turned the laptop towards Palki, opening the 'About us' page. She looked closely, for finally the name had a face: Haasil Sinha. He was traditionally good-looking. Someone who could do no wrong. Pallavi turned the laptop towards herself and continued, 'You guys were madly in love since your teenage years. And how did I come into the picture? I was in love with Haasil as well. Right from my teens. In fact, the day I got my first period was the day when my heart broke knowing Haasil had you in his life. I saw him kissing you in the rain. I don't think I can ever forget the sight. It's as if my soul has captured it forever. I eventually moved on and so did you guys. At that point in time, only Haasil knew me. I never met you before this.' Pallavi braced herself for now the lies were going to start.

'All was going well between you both. You got married as well. I did a little check. Your parents are no more now.' Before Pallavi opened a picture of her parents, she noticed a twitch in Palki's eyes. Palki took some time to check the picture. Then Pallavi said, 'Nine years ago, Haasil had opened a cloud kitchen start-up business. He wanted to do something solo, though he did take you on as a partner. When Haasil wanted to turn the cloud kitchen into a restaurant, he took a loan from a private party in Haryana. Haasil's dreams were big but the execution didn't go as per plan. The restaurant did open but . . .' Pallavi turned the laptop towards Palki again. She saw the document that was open had the name of the restaurant at the top—Divine Flavours—while the document was a balance sheet.

Pallavi went on. 'Soon the loan sharks wanted their money back. And with interest. Haasil did try to buy time but they didn't listen. He did discuss it a lot with you, especially about your share of the company. He thought he would sell off your equity to an investor and give the money to the loan sharks. But you didn't agree. Haasil couldn't pay off the loan even after a year of the sharks pestering him, and even giving him death threats. Perhaps to instil fear. You can check the balance sheet later to know the details if you want to. By then, Haasil understood time was really short. He had to do something. And he did.' Pallavi took a deep breath. This was the moment. If Palki believed this, everything else in the plan would fall into place. Pallavi braced herself and said, 'Kill the one thing that was most dear to him. His beloved. You!'

Pallavi paused to gauge Palki's reaction. Nothing major came physically. But her eyes told her it must have hit Palki a little too hard. Just as Pallavi wanted it to.

'The accident, as the world knows, wasn't an accident. It was a planned murder except he, too, had to suffer its consequences. Haasil, too, had amnesia but unlike you, he had a few memories of your past together, and only the present until the accident had been wiped off. The rest of it he regained over time.'

Palki sat in silence for some time. She couldn't believe she was the victim of a betrayal.

'But why did he try to kill me?' Palki asked. Pallavi was glad she asked that. For her homework was ready.

'The cliched insurance trope. But guess what, it worked. He had a Rs 10-crore insurance on you beforehand. That was the principal amount he had borrowed from the loan sharks. After killing you, or so he thought, Haasil paid the 10 crore with the insurance money and the interest within a year from his consulting business.' Pallavi leant forward and, with few taps on her laptop, brought up the insurance PDF. Pallavi's words matched with what Palki saw on the screen. The amount was claimed by Haasil and duly transferred to his account with an official email from the insurance company. Pallavi had dotted her i's well.

The insurance part was correct. Haasil did have an insurance cover of Rs 10 crore on Palki but his intention to claim it came only a few years after the insurance company was confident Palki wasn't going to return. But the start-up restaurant part was a white lie that Pallavi had concocted with false supporting documents.

'How do you know all of this?' Palki asked. During the next half hour, Pallavi told her another set of truths with minor lies. That Nitin had substituted her for Palki before Haasil who had memory problems. But she got to know about his ugly side too soon and left him, confessing she wasn't Palki.

'I just thought I had got my teenage love back but who wants to settle down with a cold-blooded murderer? I discovered this side of him only after staying with him as you for a brief period.'

Palki kept going through the documents on the laptop. Pallavi sat maintaining her composure, but observed her closely. Palki asked, 'Where is he now?'

'Enjoying life. Married one of his office flings, Swadha Kashyap. They are in Gurugram itself. They were living in Singapore before this. Honeymooned in the Maldives.' Pallavi intentionally added that. She knew this information would further singe Palki's image of Haasil. She had pulled out all the information about Haasil and Swadha in the last week itself, employing a private detective. Next, Pallavi showed her some of Haasil-Swadha's social media posts. They looked happy. They looked complete. Something burnt within Palki seeing them together.

Palki didn't say anything after that. Not even that night. It was during their breakfast the following morning that she told Pallavi, 'Do you think Haasil deserves to remain happy?'

And Pallavi knew her lies had worked. *Exactly my question,* Pallavi thought. Now, at present, as she stood beside Palki, after Haasil had left promising Palki that he would be divorcing Swadha soon, Palki turned to look at her.

'We are doing good, right?' she asked.

'We are doing great. Pretty much there. Haasil Sinha will fuck his own life with his own hands. Real soon,' Pallavi said and came to hug Palki.

'And we shall be there to clap,' she whispered in her ear.

Chapter 10

It wasn't that Palki took everything Pallavi had said at face
value. There were documents that Pallavi had shown her
to support her claims. At that point in time, Palki had no
option but to trust her. And she did. Till she met Haasil.
Her appearing in front of his car on her birthday was also
planned by Pallavi.

When Haasil started frequenting her place, there were
moments when Palki did casually slide in between their
conversations about the insurance money and the restaurant
start-up. While Haasil confirmed about the insurance money,
he seemed oblivious about the restaurant start-up. When
Palki asked Pallavi about it, the latter had an answer ready.

'Do you see the dichotomy?' Pallavi said. 'Knowing well
you don't remember much, he is intentionally not mentioning
the start-up so nothing leads you to the fiasco that followed
after setting it up. And he knows you can't ask Nitin about it.'

'Can't I meet Nitin once?' a gullible Palki asked.

'We can, but Nitin won't keep it to himself that you had met and asked him about the start-up. It will reach Haasil and he will know you perhaps either remember the past and are pretending to be unaware of it or someone has filled you in on the past truth. My cover will be blown along with our plan.' She deliberately brought it out as 'our' plan, for inclusiveness would make it personal for Palki.

'Why is Haasil meeting me now and pretending to love me?'

'Wait a minute. Do you think Haasil hated you? I'm sorry if what I told you presented the love story that way. He never hated you. He was totally in love with you. But the start-up fiasco revealed that he loved himself more than you. The fact that he tried killing you to cover his own ass proves that. And why is he pretending to love you now? He isn't pretending, let me tell you.'

Palki shot a sharp glance at Pallavi, who continued.

'It's his guilt that is making him come back to you even though he is already married. He is redeeming himself in front of his own self by doing this. He isn't an evil man. He is a man who chose to be evil at a certain moment. And now he wants you in his life again. Why do you think he lied about his marriage if he was a guy with a clear soul? But do you want to belong to a man like him who trades you for his own life whenever an opportunity arises?' Pallavi felt proud of the way she had twisted the perspective for Palki. The latter's face told her she was finally convinced Haasil had to be taught a lesson, for nothing could justify the betrayal.

'You're right. No woman is a toy that her man can play with and then come back whenever it's convenient for him,' Palki murmured, but Pallavi heard it right.

Pallavi had simply availed of the classic psychological tool of clouding someone's mind, and giving it a wrong context before that person meets a particular person. What happens next is the person with the clouded mind starts seeing the other person strictly through that context, thus never learning who he really is as a person. And that's what happened. The more Palki spent time with Haasil, the more she started interpreting his desperation to be with her as his way of assuaging his own guilt.

When Pallavi confessed to Eerav about the development during their human-diary session sitting in his hotel room in Mumbai, she couldn't help but feel proud of herself. Eerav, on the other hand, had a different view of it all.

'Don't you think it's all unnecessary?' His question took Pallavi by surprise.

'We aren't supposed to ask each other questions during confession,' she said.

'Cut that out for sometime. When I'd met you for the first time and subsequently got to know you a little, I thought here was someone who was like me. Wounded. And with your human-diary thing, I thought we would be able to heal each other.'

'Yeah, so why are you whining? We are doing just that,' Pallavi shot back.

'I am. You aren't. You are manipulating someone's life.'

'Really? And what were you doing sleeping with married women and leaving them high and dry?'

'Don't tell me you are such a dimwit to compare these two scenarios. I didn't force anyone. I didn't manipulate anyone. Seduction isn't necessarily manipulation. I didn't tell anyone any lies to the extent of taking them to a place from where they won't ever come back emotionally. You are actually committing an emotional crime.'

'Emotional crime? That's a nice term. But alas, it's not legal enough,' Pallavi said with mockery in her tone.

'I really think you should pull back your plans, Pallavi, before it's too late for a lot of people. It's not only you who is associated here. There are other people. And I can foresee a lot of terrible shit happening to everyone. Including you. Probably worse to you.'

A few silent seconds passed. Pallavi stood up, looked at Eerav and said intently, 'Nobody tells Pallavi what she should do. I'm not afraid of any consequences. And if you are referring to collaterals, then let me tell you I've lived a life being the collateral damage of Haasil-Palki's love story. If anyone does, it's me who has the moral right of damaging their life the way I want to. An eye for an eye.'

'Makes everyone blind,' Eerav completed it and continued, 'and what's this moral right to damage their life? You're out of your mind, Pallavi.'

Pallavi smirked. 'Not mind alone. Out of your room. And life too.' Pallavi walked to the door, moved out and pulled it closed with a loud thud.

* * *

A fortnight after Haasil had forcefully taken Swadha in their bedroom, she found herself in the office washroom holding the pregnancy toolkit in one hand and waiting to see if there was another stick line indicating her pregnancy. She had missed her periods when she was least expecting it.

Without telling Haasil about it, she called up her gynaecologist. The latter recommended a beta-hCG test.

But Swadha couldn't wait any longer. She bought the pregnancy toolkit on her way to office. She couldn't help but cry and smile together seeing the parallel line appearing on the device. She was indeed pregnant. Before she could experience the happiness fully, there was a barrage of messages on her phone. She picked it up and noticed they were images sent to her via WhatsApp from a number that hadn't been saved on her phone. She opened it. As she tapped on the hazy-looking images, they started downloading. Once they did, Swadha thought her dream had turned into a nightmare. The images were of Haasil with a woman.

And Swadha knew who the woman was.

* * *

Chapter 11

Pallavi rarely let Palki move out alone. Of course, when she accompanied Haasil, she did go out with him but otherwise Palki was more in an unstated house arrest kind of situation. Not that she blamed Pallavi for it. After all, Pallavi was the one who had brought her here, connected her to her real life, her past. She was more than indebted to Pallavi to have any complaint against her.

When Palki felt like taking some fresh air on her own and going for a little shopping, she did take Pallavi's permission to go out. That day Palki took the Uber cab booked by Pallavi to go to Connaught Place. She strolled the lanes there aimlessly, wondering if she had come there before as well. She bought a book from one of the roadside vendors and sat at a café reading it. In between sipping her coffee, she did wonder how moments like these made her feel absolutely helpless. As if she was just a doll with a beating heart. *Are humans only a set of information that they store in their brain?* she wondered. What if their brain was hampered a bit? Do they lose what they basically are? One episode of amnesia and she didn't remember her choices, her preferences, her priorities. One based everything on the information that one had collected all one's life to make choices, to take important decisions. But at present, Palki was what Pallavi had told her she was. It frustrated her.

Whenever she was with Haasil, she did try to remember the past, their once-upon-a-time marriage or even the loan fiasco that Pallavi had told her about, but she could recall nothing. It made her weep at times, but she realized life had given her another chance via Pallavi. If she looked back, it was a series of serendipitous occurrences: she being saved by Hariharan, she being taken to the fair by Sumati, she being clicked there by Mahesh and finally she being sought out by Pallavi after seeing the photograph. But what were these occurrences leading her to? Only Haasil's destruction? Revenge couldn't be anyone's lifelong goal, Palki thought. What would her life be like after executing the collective plan of destroying Haasil? Palki had no clue. Maybe she would have to redesign her life then. Perhaps in her own way. Maybe then she would have some power to choose how she wanted to be. With whom she wanted to be surrounded by. And finally live a little on her own terms.

After finishing her coffee, Palki went shopping. She used the money she had earned as a model for Mahesh. Then she strolled by different blocks in the area, sucking on an ice cream, looking around inquisitively. Till she reached a particular block. She remembered Pallavi had told her that Haasil had opened the restaurant somewhere there. She felt an impulse to know about it. *What if I meet someone who knows more than what Pallavi told me?* She did try to squeeze Haasil about the restaurant but he never shared anything.

He pretended as if nothing of the sort happened. Or so Palki thought. Little did she know that he didn't share about the restaurant because nothing of that sort had ever happened for real.

Palki went around to different shops in the block and inquired about the restaurant. No one seemed to know it. Palki concluded that perhaps it was years ago and the fact that it never ran for long was why it had not made it to anyone's memory.

Disappointed that she couldn't collect any information about the restaurant, Palki continued to window-shop for an hour more, after which she called Pallavi and requested her to book an Uber for her. While waiting for the cab, Palki had put on her AirPods, listening to some soft music, distracting herself in the process. She was continuously looking at the left side of the lane, expecting the cab to turn up from there. Out of nowhere, a car came up, dangerously close, from the right side of the lane. It was only her instinct that made her glance to her right at the last moment. Realizing the car was too close for comfort, she took some hurried steps back and collapsed on the ground.

One look up at the speeding car, and Palki noticed its model—Maybach—and the car's number as well. She had seen it quite a few times before, whenever Haasil came to meet her in it.

* * *

BOOK 3: The Game of Love

Chapter 1

At first Swadha was in denial mode for some hours. *Of course it's a prank*, she kept telling herself. Though the pictures were auto-saved in her phone, she was scared to even see them the second time. *What if they were real?* The images, though, were vibrant in her mind all through the day. They robbed her focus at work. In the end, after office, Swadha went out alone to a pub and ordered a mocktail, knowing well that alcohol may damage her pregnancy, and sat down to check the pictures properly. To confront what scares you is the first step to neutralizing the fear.

Swadha magnified the photographs on her phone screen—one at a time. She literally checked every pixel in them. Her mind was sure they weren't Photoshopped but her heart wasn't ready to accept the fact. Being emotionally edgy, Swadha ended up ordering a small peg of whisky. She needed to steady herself.

Once Swadha sipped a little of the whisky on the rocks, she decided to call the number from which the pictures had come. She called it not once but several times, but was told by an automated voice that it was switched off. She tried Truecaller to check the name but that too didn't get her any conclusive results. With shaky hands, she left a message: *Who's this?* But it was not delivered.

When Swadha went home, she couldn't help but notice Haasil's actions acutely. The pictures had suddenly turned her eyes into a magnifying glass. Especially when they were on Haasil. But watching him minutely, Swadha soon realized there was nothing much she could pinpoint. He was his usual self. No untoward behaviour. Or was his usual self an illusion? Swadha hated herself for suspecting Haasil on the basis of some pictures. They weren't intimate ones, but the chemistry . . . and that face . . . it didn't make any sense to her. *Why would Haasil go back to Pallavi*, Swadha wondered. *Someone's bullshitting for sure*, she concluded. Though the pictures were of Palki and Haasil, when Pallavi had sent them to Swadha, she knew the latter would assume it was her. Palki, for the world, was dead.

It was in the dead of night, after seeing her message was delivered and read, that Swadha called the number again. It rang but nobody picked up. Swadha called again. Four times straight. And then it was picked up on the fifth attempt.

'Hello? Anyone there? Hello?' Swadha could hear light breathing from the other end, but there was no voice.

'Why did you send me those pictures?' Swadha kept asking the same question. Then she said, 'I want to meet you.' Pallavi ended the call the next second. She had guessed Swadha would want to do that. She was even ready if Swadha first showed the pictures to Haasil but it would have meant, apart from Haasil being curious about who the sender could be, that Haasil's life was further fucked.

Pallavi messaged Swadha two days later and called her to a hookah bar during the daytime. Swadha was quick to cancel all her work meetings only to reach there on time.

Once in the bar, Swadha was ushered to where Pallavi was waiting for her. As the smoke of the hookah diffused, Swadha saw her face. It had the same arrogance she had seen the day she had asked her to buzz off from Haasil's life years ago. Time had not touched her much. Though things were different now, Swadha still felt Pallavi looked more confident than her.

Swadha sat down opposite her. Their eyes had the conversation for the first few minutes, as Pallavi continued to drag from her hookah.

'So, you wanted to meet, huh?' Pallavi said.

'Why did you send me those pictures?' Swadha asked. Pallavi felt like laughing her ass off. *She couldn't possibly be that innocent,* she wondered and said, 'So that you know the truth.'

'What if I say I don't believe you?' Swadha wanted to see something more conclusive. Pallavi unlocked her phone and turned it forward to her. Swadha took it, saw the screen had a WhatsApp chat with someone whose name was saved as Haasil. The display picture was the same as Haasil's current WhatsApp DP. She immediately checked the phone number. It was Haasil's. Feeling a few knots in her stomach, Swadha did try to read the chat but the kiss emojis made her drop the phone on the table. Pallavi took the phone back and kept it beside her. Swadha didn't have to know the phone was actually Palki's.

'There's something else I think you should see as well,' Pallavi said and took out another phone. It was hers. She tapped on it a few times and gave it to Swadha—who couldn't believe her eyes. There were medical reports of Haasil, dated a year ago. And some belonged to the present year. She didn't need any help to know those were his semen analysis reports which she guessed weren't of the desired results. But the ones in front of her pitched Haasil's semen analysis as perfect. *Whom does she believe now?* Swadha wondered and asked, 'How did you get these?'

Pallavi drew her attention to the phone to show her where the email had come from. Swadha's eyes widened in shock on seeing Haasil's email ID.

'Years ago, when I was in Haasil's life as Palki, I'd made sure I saved my email ID on his forwarding emails. The usual possessive bitch that I was. That I am. Of course, I didn't know then that I would be out of his life or that he would be back in my life again.'

That was the only piece of truth Pallavi gave Swadha. She had indeed saved her email ID on Haasil's forwarding email years ago. It was something Haasil neither knew nor had a suspicion of even after he had ousted Pallavi from his life. After breaking up with her, Haasil did change all his passwords but he didn't know she was still getting his emails. That was also how Pallavi had secured the insurance policy documents and a few others to show Palki while narrating her fabricated story.

'Now, if you are wondering why I showed all this to you, the answer is simple and the same that I'd told you years ago as well. Haasil doesn't have the courage to tell you about our affair, so I had to make you aware. Swadha Kashyap, my proposition remains the same. Please fuck off from Haasil's life. This time for your own good, really,' Pallavi said, put a few currency notes on the table, her bill for the hookah, and walked off with an air of arrogance as if she were Haasil's wife while Swadha was the other woman in his life.

Swadha, for the longest time, couldn't move. She desperately wanted someone to tell her that all this was a nightmare, starting from her getting the pictures to meeting Pallavi in person. Nobody came.

Pallavi felt jubilant while driving to her place because she had just made sure she had fucked Haasil's life further. Swadha would go home and confront Haasil. Pallavi was anticipating that Swadha would tell Haasil about her but she couldn't care less even if he knew about her now. Or her plan. He would not be able to shrug off the injury that she had set him up for.

Revelling in the pleasure of imagining Haasil's tormented face once Swadha told him that she knew about his affair, Pallavi smiled to herself. During a traffic-signal stop, she took her phone out and tapped a button to check on Palki. As the room's camera feed opened up, Pallavi's smile disappeared. It seemed she was on happy-high and someone had bitch-slapped her out of it. Her phone had the feed of the room where Palki was. She wasn't alone. Haasil was all over her, their naked bodies covered with a blanket. For the first time, they were making love. Urgent, desperate, passionate love. It wasn't part of her plan. Nor would Palki tell her about it. Pallavi couldn't stop the feed or avert her eyes. Her core within seemed frozen. Seeing the visual, a feeling took premature birth inside her. And it told her if Swadha had taken what was Palki's, the latter was experiencing what was . . . Pallavi's. And it wasn't the best of feelings.

Pallavi punched the car's windowpane impulsively, with all her might. It caused a small crack in the glass and made her fingers bleed mildly. But that was not the only part bleeding.

Chapter 2

From the time Pallavi had first brought Palki to the previous rented place and then to the present one, she had installed hidden cameras all over the flat. Palki was a tool for her. And she couldn't afford to keep her away from her eyes. Especially when she had to fly out of Delhi for work. Palki was completely unaware of the fact that she was being monitored 24/7.

Pallavi anxiously waited outside the house till she saw Haasil drive off in his Maybach. One glance at the camera feed on her phone and she noticed Palki crying in her room. A few minutes later, Pallavi went inside.

'He was here,' Palki said, the moment she saw Pallavi stepping in. Updating everything she shared with Haasil to Pallavi had become a ritual for Palki. It was evident to Pallavi that Palki had wiped her tears pretty roughly. There were faint smudge marks on her cheeks.

'And . . .?' Pallavi didn't make anything obvious. She only sat down on the sofa with as casual an air as she could manage though her heart hadn't stopped beating hard since she saw the two making love. Palki came close to her.

'We made love for the first time. You were right. I can't believe a man who tried to kill me before, even recently, had the audacity to make love to me with such warmth.'

Palki held Pallavi tight and broke down.

'I was so confused. I wanted to hate him for whatever shit he'd done to me but I simply couldn't. The moment his lips touched mine, everything seemed false,' Palki spoke as she sobbed. Pallavi didn't interrupt her. When she lifted her head, Pallavi noticed a deep love bite on her bosom. Palki felt a little uncomfortable. Pallavi felt destroyed. For her it was a sign of claiming someone. Her jaws locked.

'I'm sorry. I won't let this happen again,' Palki said in an apologetic tone.

'It's all right,' Pallavi released her jaws as she spoke with a certain conclusiveness in her voice. 'Just make sure you don't let him see this vulnerable side of yours. Else . . .'

'I won't,' Palki said, as Pallavi got up to go to the washroom. But what she couldn't see or hear was that Pallavi had opened the tap in full force to mute her own weeping. After a long time, Pallavi's tears were mocking her own self.

From the next day onwards, Palki found Haasil telling her more of their past with an unprecedented fervour. As if he was on a mission to make her aware of whatever nature had erased. He told her about the times when they were together before the accident. He brought photographs with him and narrated the moments in detail leading to the clicks. Seeing Haasil's actions, Palki understood that what Pallavi had told her was correct. That Haasil wasn't a bad man. Just that he'd put himself over her when it came to saving himself. The moment she started asking about the restaurant, he made sure he threatened her by trying to run her over with his car. What did he think, she wouldn't recognize his car? It was also clear to her that perhaps Haasil was stalking her. Did that kind of man deserve her love again? Or anyone's love? It was constant food for thought for her.

Palki intentionally started avoiding meeting him at the rented place. The lovemaking episode had somewhere left a bad emotional taste. Not because the act itself wasn't good. In fact, it was as good as it could be but the confusing feelings it generated in her was what Palki wasn't ready for. Nor knew how to handle. Somewhere, she thought, it made her weak.

When Haasil proposed a travel plan, Palki rejected it outright.

'It's your official travel. It's better you go alone, Haasil.'

'But we can fly together. Put up at the same hotel. I'll finish my work in one day, then we can spend a couple of days together,' Haasil seemed excited.

'Do you realize, Haasil, how from being an open book in front of everyone, we have now become each other's secret?' There was pain in Palki's voice. It was genuine, though. There had been times when Palki felt the pangs of jealousy, of envy and she didn't like those feelings one bit. It didn't come naturally to her. But she couldn't weed them out either. Everything Swadha was experiencing was hers. Including her man. What was she supposed to do? Just accept things as they were? Oh yes, life had played a bitch and turned things this way. So be quiet and move on to being Haasil's mistress now. The thought used to tear Palki apart from within. She did think of sharing these with Pallavi but the kind of person Palki was, she preferred to keep it all within her. Venting wasn't her priority or nature. But regaining her lost life, if possible without harming anyone, was what she was seeking deep within.

'I know,' Haasil said guiltily.

'You don't know shit. Just imagine you coming back into your wife's life and seeing her with another man. And then she makes you her three-hours-a-day acquaintance. Would you want to secretly travel with her when her husband isn't around? How would you feel? Won't your self-respect stop you? Maul you from the inside? It's not about what I or you want any more, Haasil. Yeah, we can make love daily, just like we did the other day, we can date secretly, travel secretly and carry on doing this forever without your present wife getting to know. But is this the status we want for our relationship? For a relationship that is older than your present marriage?'

Palki turned her face away after the monologue. Haasil realized she would be moist-eyed. He couldn't even say she was wrong. Every word she said was correct. This was one reason why he took his time to become physically intimate with her. Doesn't matter what people say, physical intimacy has its own hangover after an emotional connection.

'You're right, Palki. I think it's high time I take a call. I don't want to hide anything from you. Somewhere, living distantly with Swadha and meeting you outside had become a comfort zone for me.' Comfort zones are tricky in a dangerous way. They make you believe what's happening is good. And thus you carry on with it. But when someone shows you the mirror, like Palki just did to him, you understand that what has been happening is a waste of life.

'Next time we meet,' Haasil stood up and said, 'Swadha would know about us. We won't be yours, mine or anyone's secret any more.' It sounded like a conclusive announcement.

Haasil left. *Hide anything from you*, Palki wondered as his words ricocheted within her. *The authenticity with which Haasil said it*, Palki thought, *if I had not known his reality, I would have actually believed him.*

When Pallavi visited her in the evening, Palki's first question to her was simple yet direct.

'What's next in our plan?'

Pallavi stared at Palki for few seconds longer than usual. And said, 'Something from which he would never be able to make a comeback.' *Nor you*, she thought.

Chapter 3

It took Sanjana by surprise when Swadha asked for a cigarette. They had gone to swim in the sports club together. They showered, freshened up and were heading towards their parked cars when Swadha made her request. Sanjana was quick to offer her one. She too lit one up. A few seconds later, she noticed Swadha was mouth-fagging but she didn't interrupt her for Swadha looked jittery.

'What is it?' Sanjana asked. 'You looked a little off at the swim too.'

While Sanjana had completed her laps in her usual time, Swadha had taken nearly double her normal time to do the same.

'Haasil is having an affair,' Swadha said, straight-faced, as if she still hadn't accepted the truth. Sanjana was visibly shocked. She took her time to take her next drag after hearing this. The fact that Swadha had not mentioned the lady, she understood perhaps she wanted to keep her out of it.

'Are you sure?' Sanjana chose her words carefully. And saw Swadha nodding.

'Dead sure.'

The way the words came out, from between her clenched teeth, Sanjana knew she had seen evidence of it.

'Did you talk to him?'

Swadha shook her head and then took her time before speaking.

'I wanted to. Catch him by the collar and ask him straight what the fuck is wrong with him or what's his need to compromise our marriage like this. But I didn't. I don't want to confront him. He is the one who is having an affair. He needs to tell me.' After a pause, she added, 'If he thinks I'm important enough.' A tear trickled down her cheek. She walked to a dustbin, extinguished the leftover cigarette against its body and threw it inside. Sanjana did the same.

'Till then, things will go on like before with some difference,' Swadha said. She climbed inside her car, started it and then popped her head out to say, 'I just wanted someone to know this. Please don't share this with Nitin.'

'I understand. And I won't,' Sanjana said. Swadha drove out of the sports club.

From that night onwards, Swadha started being the one who behaved in an aloof manner. Like Haasil had been for months now. It was difficult for her for she had understood it clearly that she loved Haasil more than he loved her. Not that she had a problem with it. It just meant her suffering would be more than his if anything in their relationship went wrong. And as things stood, almost everything had gone wrong. Perhaps irreparably.

Swadha went to the extent of packing her bags and keeping them ready so she could leave any moment he confessed about the affair. But he didn't. And it damaged her further. To her, it only meant she wasn't pertinent to him. Haasil did notice the packed bags but didn't ask about them. There were times when she did ask Haasil, 'Do you want to share anything?' He didn't. It made him a little curious, yet he didn't.

Swadha didn't tell him but she did apply via LinkedIn for the post of managing director at a Delhi-based start-up. But the delay in Haasil's confession made her question her own self. *Where had she fallen short in her attempts?* And then one night, the words of her friend Arpita, whom she had met in Singapore a few years back, came back to her. Her husband had told her he had fallen out of love with her even though she had given her heart and soul to the marriage.

She kept pondering over her possible shortcomings day in and day out till one night, after Haasil had promised Palki that he would tell Swadha about them, he came home in an unprecedented inebriated state. He was finding it difficult to even stand straight when Swadha opened the door for him. She gave him support and was trying to take him to the bedroom when he said he wanted to sit on the couch in the hall and talk to her. Swadha made him sit down, realizing he wouldn't agree to anything otherwise.

'I want to tell you something, Swadha,' he said, looking everywhere else but at her.

Was this the moment? Swadha dreaded it. Her heart started beating harder and faster. *Was their marriage destined to live till this moment?* A part of her wanted to disappear while a part of her desired to hear it; once and for all. That he was having an . . .

'I think we aren't compatible. We should look ahead and let each other live in peace,' Haasil managed to mumble though Swadha heard him clearly. Her heart sank.

Was she in love with a man who couldn't even look straight into her eyes and tell her he had another woman in his life? She would have respected him more even though then, too, she would have left him. But in that scenario, she would have left him knowing that somewhere she was important enough for him to share the truth. And not some half-baked flimsy excuse only to part ways. Had she been in love with a coward of a man all along or was it their marriage that had turned him into one? The emotional whirlwind Swadha was experiencing within made her clench her fists tight. As if she wanted to switch to physical violence to release her deep-seated anger. And hurt.

Swadha, who was sitting opposite him on the other couch, stood up, came close and slapped him hard. Haasil fell back on the couch and passed out. Swadha wanted to scream all the toxicity out of her lungs. But she quietly went to the bedroom. And locked the door behind her.

Chapter 4

When the staff at the reception of The Lalit, Mumbai, called her room and told Pallavi that someone by the name of Eerav wanted to meet her, a victorious smile spread on her face. That's how Pallavi always was. Everything was about winning or failing. And since her teens, she knew well which side gave her the high. Eerav's coming back to her without her calling him told her he must have missed her, must have realized his mistake and was here to make a truce. She was soon going to find out how wrong she was.

Pallavi told the reception staff to send Eerav up to her room. Half a minute later, the staff called back saying Eerav wanted to meet her downstairs in the lobby.

'The gentleman said he is waiting here, ma'am.'

'Attitude, huh?' Pallavi said and took some time to move out of the room. While going down in the glass elevator, she noticed Eerav gently pacing up and down in the lobby. Instead of his clean-shaven look, he was now sporting a slight stubble.

'Hey!' she said, approaching him. Eerav turned to look at her.

'Hey! Sorry if I'm disturbing you . . .'

'Thanks for stabbing me with the formality, dude,' Pallavi said.

'Nothing like that,' Eerav said. 'I know we haven't been in touch since a long time.'

'Yeah, you acted funny.' Pallavi made it sound as though their break-up was his fault.

Eerav handed over an envelope to her. Pallavi took it with heightened curiosity.

Eerav gave her a wry smile as he spoke. 'Whether you'll believe it or not, you have been an important person in my life. Someone I can never forget. Not because of what you did to my life but what I understood about my own life after learning about yours. Healmate of sorts, as you'd put it. And perhaps we don't connect any more because one of us has healed.'

Pallavi looked up at Eerav once he finished. Till then she had perused every corner of the card that had been in the envelope. *Eerav Weds Kavya*, it read. The marriage was to take place in three months in Udaipur. A destination wedding. Pallavi didn't say anything. The silence made the entire rendezvous awkward. The fact that he hadn't told her anything about the marriage till the cards were ready told Pallavi that her walk-off from the hotel room the last time they met, must have hurt him more than she had fathomed. Eerav took the silence as his lead to leave.

'I hope to see you in Udaipur. Take care,' he said and turned but she stopped him.

'Congrats. For the healing, I mean,' she said.

'Thanks.'

'Don't you dare ghost her,' Pallavi said with a sarcastic smile. Eerav joined in the smile.

'Coffee?' she asked.

Eerav seemed to be in two minds.

'Don't worry, I no longer indulge myself in men who are taken,' Pallavi said with a hint of irony.

'Oh, really? Then who the hell is Haasil?'

'He has always been mine. It's just that he hasn't agreed yet.'

Eerav found it amusing that Pallavi could joke about it. Or at least it seemed so to him.

'Yeah, right. Before you throw more irony at me, let's just have the goddamn coffee,' he said.

Half an hour later, they were taking the last sips of their coffee when Pallavi suddenly spoke up, 'Okay, enough of this twaddle. Now that my human diary is never going to come back to me, let me share one last confession.'

'All ears, like old times. Remember this is the last page of the diary. Make the confession worth it,' Eerav said.

'All right, I think even I'm done. For the last few weeks I've been toying with the idea of settling down.'

Eerav gave her a surprised-out-of-his-wits look.

'Not in the traditional sense. Settling down as in I think it's time I do things for myself. Keep myself at the core of my life. My mistake was I'd kept Haasil as my life's core. And whatever I did from there on was either to hurt him, injure him or snatch things from him. These days I'm wondering, when will I live for myself?'

'I'm so happy that you've finally decided to focus on your own self. I think we both had got it wrong. After our heartbreaks we thought we were moving on, but we kept thinking about the one from whom we were supposed to move on. So the entire exercise became futile. It was like running in a circle, really.'

'Precisely.'

'This was what I was trying to explain to you the last time we met. What would you get by harming others? Happiness? The nickname to such happiness is self-bullshitting.'

'So, now I've decided to do things which are only about me.'

Sometime later, Eerav finally got up to leave. They hugged tightly. She promised him that she would be there in Udaipur for the wedding.

Pallavi headed back to her room feeling light. She had wanted to urgently share her thoughts of settling down with someone. And Eerav was just the kind of serendipity she was wishing for. She went inside her room, entered the washroom and stripped bare. She stood in front of the mirror. Then turned to look into the oval magnifying face mirror, where all the minute lines of her face were pronounced. Pallavi realized one should have both the normal and magnifying mirrors in one's life. She was looking at the normal one till date but the moment she saw Palki and Haasil's lovemaking feed, it was as if the magnifying mirror appeared and showed her the details of her wounded feelings. And in it she realized there was something more important in life than damaging Haasil. It was about healing herself. It was a simple truth but she had to go through a long, shitty road to get to this point.

Pallavi picked up her phone from the shelf in front of her. She opened the lovemaking video of Haasil and Palki, which she had saved after going through it several times since she saw it the first time. She placed the phone, with the video playing, in a way so she could see it from the shower. She went to stand under the shower and started masturbating looking at the video and thinking about her and . . . her life's core. As promised to Eerav she would, from now on, focus on herself. And her own self was all about Haasil Sinha. A few minutes later, her body shuddered with an orgasm.

Chapter 5

Haasil knew his subtle confession about the divorce neither came out properly nor was the way he chose to do it, being drunk, the right way of going about it. The next morning, he did try to talk again but got no response from Swadha. *She needs some time*, he thought and prepared himself for that. The one who loved the other more needed more time to accept the end of the relationship, Haasil knew. He relayed the same to Palki but there, too, he got silence as a response. He knew both the silences had a different meaning. Swadha's silence was more because of an injured self-respect. And her silence was so loud that Haasil could hear it every time she was around, be it at home or in the office. While Palki's silence was inquiring in nature, questioning whether a togetherness with him was ever possible again.

Haasil tried his best to initiate a conversation with Swadha whenever a situation surfaced. Deep within, he knew the silence wouldn't lead them anywhere except for wasting time. And the more time he spent with Swadha, he knew well, the more Palki would be convinced he wasn't serious about the whole thing. What frustrated him was that earlier, when he would ignore Swadha, she would be hell-bent on talking to him. Now, when he wanted to talk, she was maintaining a stoic silence. As if none of his attempts registered with her. As if she had built this emotional insulation from him.

On the other side, Swadha knew well what Haasil was up to. He would, *just* like any other man, convince her that their love story was over. *Just* like any other man, he would make her believe he deserved someone better. *Just* like any other man, he demanded acceptance from his woman, no matter how unjustified it was.

The pain, though, was in the fact that Swadha, *just* like any other woman-in-love, all through her life with him, thought he wasn't *just* any other man. And now she knew, especially after he came out with the stupid incompatibility excuse, that he, too, was just like any other man. For the first time since Haasil had proposed marriage to her years ago she wondered, would it have been better if her most treasured dream, her most prized fantasy had never come true? There's no sadder plight than when life makes you discover the ordinary side of the person you thought was extraordinary.

Swadha, again, messaged Pallavi on the number she'd sent the photographs from, asking her to meet one last time. A day later, Pallavi's response came that she was okay with meeting her. This time Swadha picked her up in her car from outside a metro station. The two ladies talked while driving around. By then, Pallavi had understood Swadha had not yet confronted Haasil about meeting her. That, too, worked for her. Though the reason for it eluded her.

'Don't tell me to talk to Haasil. That won't be possible.' Pallavi had pondered why Swadha would want to meet her again. And one of the top reasons she could surmise was perhaps she wanted her to talk Haasil out of the affair. A pleading of sorts. When Swadha spoke next, Pallavi realized it was something she didn't have in her assumption list.

'I just wanted to know what made Haasil come back to you. As far as I know, he hated you. Why this sudden change?'

'Do I really need to tell you that?'

'It's important for my closure. Haasil told me we are incompatible. I don't understand how two people can suddenly turn incompatible. If we were so, we both would have known it in the first or maximum two years of marriage. Neither is he a fool nor am I.'

'Hmm, he lied. It's not about your incompatibility.'

'I guessed so. Hence I'm here,' Swadha said.

'I never asked him why exactly he came to me, nor did he ever clarify. In fact, we never discussed you.' There was a condescending tone in the last statement. Swadha did catch it, and glanced at her once before looking ahead at the road. Pallavi had taken a quick decision sitting beside her. She would have to damage Swadha enough so that she never came back to her. She would have to make it clear that she didn't possess any further answers. Pallavi couldn't afford to meet Swadha again and again.

'You know, Swadha, there are people who can only love someone but can't hold on to them. I don't know if you have come across such people but I have. There's this friend who loves her husband crazily but her process to express her love is so mundane that her husband claims he never found any love with her. It doesn't mean they didn't love each other ever, but in a relationship, one needs to have the glimpse of love in the other person in some form or the other. Else people drift away. I think that's what happened to Haasil. Maybe he never saw your love for him. Or somehow it didn't reach him.'

Is she kidding me? Swadha wondered. *I did everything in my power to show Haasil, on a daily basis, that I loved him. Or how much he meant to me. How can he, or anyone, be blind to that? Or is it . . .*

'But I've done my best always, how can he . . .'

'In that case, you know the obvious,' Pallavi cut her short. Swadha could sense a rise in her heartbeat. *The obvious?* She slowed down and parked her car at a random spot.

'What's the obvious?' she asked.

'That Haasil never loved you. Perhaps you were his temporary emotional furniture to feel comfortable. I was his home.' Pallavi made it as subtly acidic as she could. Swadha didn't speak after that. Pallavi understood she wouldn't. She got out and left.

Sitting alone in her car, Swadha broke down. It was a catharsis. A beggar came and knocked at her window but seeing her state walked away, blessing her. *So, that was it?* she thought. *I was emotional furniture?* What was worse was Pallavi's words made sense to her. If she wasn't what Pallavi told her, Haasil wouldn't have distanced himself from her so easily. Wouldn't have given her that shit of an excuse of incompatibility. Most importantly, when one of the two compromises on something that both have built with compassion, sweat and time, then the guilty one, in the least, owes the other an explanation if not an apology. In a relationship that is breaking apart, an explanation is way more therapeutic, but underused and underhyped, than a mere apology.

Swadha wiped her tears, picked up her phone and called Sanjana. She picked up at the third ring.

'What's the number of that gynae you went to for an abortion?' Swadha had never sounded so cold before.

Chapter 6

Though Sanjana tried her best to convince Swadha not to abort the child, Swadha was in no mood to listen.

'My situation was different, darl. I didn't want it. Yours is different. You bloody want a child,' Sanjana said. She went on and on and on but when nothing affected Swadha, Sanjana too gave up. She understood the emotionally edgy side of her was a direct consequence of Haasil's extramarital affair.

'Let me coordinate it,' Sanjana said resignedly. She took an appointment the next day with the same gynae she had gone to.

'May I know the reason for this?' the doctor asked Swadha when they met her as per the appointment. They had told her that she wanted to do away with the pregnancy.

'The child is the result of an episode of marital rape. It doesn't belong to the man I'm in love with,' Swadha blurted out. Sanjana glanced at her, shocked at her bluntness. The doctor didn't ask any further questions. She did a sonography and gave Swadha some medicines, asking her to visit her on a certain date later that month.

'Can't it happen earlier?'

'I'm out of station from tomorrow,' the doctor said. 'But don't worry, there's no risk involved even if we do it later.'

Stepping out of the clinic, Sanjana realized Swadha was a different woman. Whatever Sanjana asked her, Swadha seemed to have slowed down with her response. A clear indication of how much was going on in her mind. She dropped Swadha home.

When Swadha saw Haasil at home, she reacted as if he were a stranger. A certain formality crept into her body language as well in the words she spoke. Haasil noticed it but guessed perhaps this was her preparation to say yes to the divorce. He was surprised, though, when he saw her take her pillow and blanket and go to sleep in the other room alone. Swadha slept through the night holding on to her tummy in an apologetic manner. It seemed she was saying sorry to her unborn child for her choice of abortion.

The morning after, while Haasil was running on the treadmill kept in the deck area, Swadha came up and said, 'Let me know when you want to meet the lawyer. Let's keep it low key. I don't want anyone to know.' She left the room. Haasil had noticed she was dressed for office. A few seconds later, he heard the main door close with a thud. She had left.

Haasil stopped the treadmill, wiped his sweat and looked out at the bustling Gurugram traffic visible from the deck. Should he be happy? Or neutral? He was happy Swadha had accepted his proposal without any kind of fight. It told Haasil she was mature enough. On the other hand, he would finally get to tell Palki, looking into her eyes, that now it was a matter of time till they were together again. Just as before. It was a relief for Haasil. But he couldn't be entirely happy about it for he knew it did not matter how mature Swadha had been about it; she must be injured within.

Haasil picked up his phone and, opening his WhatsApp window with Swadha, typed: *I'm sorry but thank you.* Then he erased it. Instead, he opened Palki's WhatsApp window and typed: *Finally, we will be together. You don't have to be sad any more.* He sent it. A few moments later, Palki's response came: *What happened?* Haasil replied: *Swadha has said yes to our divorce. Let's meet today?* He received a response from Palki when he reached the office a couple of hours later.

Can't meet today. Out of station for work. Will message when back.

Haasil sighed and sent a sad emoji to Palki. He consoled himself, saying it was a matter of time now when they would live together again. It was sometime during the day when Nitin called him to check the reason for Swadha's resignation. It was a shock for Haasil, but he pretended in front of Nitin that he knew about it. In the evening, he followed Swadha out of the office and stopped her in the basement parking.

'I would have never asked you to resign because of what has happened between us,' Haasil said. Swadha looked at him, smirked and said, 'I've stopped living a life where what you want me to do matters to me any more. My only regret is I should have done this way before, when I wasn't this invested in the marriage. In a way, you have ruined the last eight years of my life.'

Haasil knew he was guilty as charged. But back then, when he had proposed to her, he didn't know Palki was about to come back into his life. If he did, he would have never married or even proposed to her. Swadha was always his plan B which he was living as if she was plan A. It was just that he could never tell her so. Not even now. He simply stood there and watched Swadha drive away.

Sanjana made sure she called Swadha every day till the date of the abortion to coax her out of it. The news was getting the better of her as well and there were times when Sanjana felt pushed enough to tell Nitin about it. But she didn't, knowing how Swadha had maintained the secrecy of her abortion. It only saddened her that no amount of persuasion could dampen Swadha's conviction.

At Swadha's end, deep within, she had accepted that till she damaged something that Haasil had gifted her, she wouldn't be at peace. She wasn't killing their child. She was killing what Haasil and she stood for. It was her comeback for his compromise of the marriage. The intention was toxic but it was an evil spell of sorts that she was living under, from the time she'd met the gynae to the time she found herself lying inside the small operation theatre in the clinic. Swadha, hitherto, had never felt so full of hatred and negativity as she did at that moment. Every second was claustrophobic, sucking the life out of her spool by spool.

The doctor told her that the abortion would be similar to giving birth. She would have to push the foetus out. Except it would be dead. It made things more difficult for her. The first time she was on the fringes of feeling like a mother, something she had been waiting for subconsciously for a long time, happened when she actually pushed a dead foetus out. Swadha passed out after she had a glimpse of it.

Haasil had no inkling of what was going on with her. He only saw Sanjana accompany Swadha home that day. He thought something was wrong with Sanjana.

'I'm good. We had some shopping plans to discuss,' Sanjana said and then took Swadha inside.

Haasil, shrugging off residual doubts, went out to meet Palki. It had been a few weeks that they hadn't met. She had told him that she was out of Delhi because of a shoot. Haasil didn't push her much because he too was having a busy month. Little did he know that Palki was in Delhi and it was only because Pallavi asked her to detach a bit from him, that Palki didn't meet Haasil. It was in the morning that Palki messaged Haasil that she was back, but she needed to talk to him about something urgently. He told her he would come to her place.

Haasil reached there, parked his car and went to Palki's house. He pressed the doorbell a few times but nobody opened it. Palki had told him before that the key was always under a flowerpot by the door. Haasil waited for some time and called her. During the second call, he felt he could hear a vague ringtone coming from inside. He pressed the doorbell a few more times. Then checked the flowerpot. The key was there. It meant she wasn't out. He decided to pick up the key and go inside.

'Palki?' he called out, looking around. There was no response. He called her again. Palki's phone ringtone was coming from the bedroom. Haasil tiptoed inside, sensing something ominous was about to happen. When he reached the bedroom, his eyes fell on Palki. She was on the floor. There was blood all around her. He noticed her hand seemed slashed. Then he saw her still fingers were clasping a note. Haasil took it out and read:

You're responsible for my death, Haasil.

And just when Haasil was about to check her heartbeat, he heard the doorbell ring.

Chapter 7

When Palki had come up to Pallavi and asked, 'What's next in our plan?', the latter too had no clue. It had all started with Pallavi wanting to wound Haasil the way she had been injured. An absolute wound from which there would be no coming back for him. A wound which would remain with him long enough to become a part of who he was and then would define him in every way possible. Just as it had happened with her. She was convinced about her actions till that one video—Palki making love to Haasil—brought into prominence a question. A very important question that had not occurred to her before. Should she only be happy by destroying Haasil or should she make sure he became hers?

The first question may have given her happiness but the latter, she knew, would bring about a peace that would be potent enough perhaps to heal her forever. Between happiness and healing, Pallavi had finally chosen healing. She knew well that to get to that healing, a lot of things had to fall into place. Not on their own but via a new plan that she had cooked up.

'You asked me so many times whether Haasil would accept he had betrayed you and tried to kill you before, right?'

Palki nodded. For her, Haasil's confession was important on two counts. One, it would put a final nail on whatever Pallavi had told her with no space for any doubt. Second, it would be an emotional closure for her now that she knew what had transpired at the accident.

'So, next is we will make Haasil confess to his betrayal of you.'

Palki couldn't contain her surprise.

'How? Every time I have tried to probe into the matter, he either ignored it or feigned as if he knew nothing about it.'

'That will end,' Pallavi said and told Palki about her plan of faking her death. She asked her to stay away from Haasil for a few weeks citing work as an excuse and then call him home. Once he was there, he would find Palki dead.

'But by faking my death, how can we make him confess?' Palki asked. A similarity in looks was one thing but what Pallavi had realized was the one major difference between them: Palki was gullible and way more simple than Pallavi. Palki understood things clearly only when they were explained to her.

Pallavi showed Palki her phone where the camera feed appeared. And it was only then that Palki understood the plan and was convinced it would compel Haasil to confess. To make sure it all looked authentic, Pallavi added the suicide note part. Basic psychology told her that, on seeing Palki dead, Haasil would be in too much of a mind-clogged state to do the obvious thing of checking her heartbeat or pulse. Especially when he saw the suicide note. Would he call the police? He might, Pallavi thought, but then he would be the prime suspect. Would he risk that? Chances were minimal. From Haasil's point of view, nobody knew about Palki's existence. In the police files, she was dead. Still, Pallavi didn't want to take a chance. She added a layer of fear-psychosis to counter Haasil's attempt to check if Palki was alive. And that's what had happened. She had him on the phone cam feed when he entered the flat. And just when she felt he was trying to check whether Palki was alive or not, she herself pressed the doorbell. She watched Haasil standing beside Palki's body in two minds. Then he left Palki the way she was on the floor and went to check who it was. Pallavi had moved away by then, keeping a tab on Haasil's movements on her phone. The fear-psychosis worked as she saw him leave the apartment hastily, looking nervous.

The plan had been executed to the T. Except Palki didn't know there was more to the plan than what she had been told. Like the car—the Maybach—which tried to run down Palki belonged to Haasil but Pallavi had bribed his driver enough for him to not only lend her the car but also to keep his mouth shut about the matter. The driver did it happily, assuming that it was Palki—the same lady he'd seen with Haasil a few times. And that there would be no harm involved.

* * *

Haasil indeed was flabbergasted. He didn't know if he should have reported Palki's suicide to the police or not. The doorbell had turned his anxiety button on. He was too blank for the first one hour. Had it been a murder, he surely would have reported it. But the note was a direct implication of him. With a blank mind, he came back home. He was visibly edgy. And when he saw Swadha had packed all her remaining belongings, his pleading mode came on. If he needed someone at the moment, it was her.

'Can't you stay here?' he asked. Swadha looked at him. One more second and she would have given in. Instead, she averted her eyes and said, 'The guard is on his way to help me with my stuff.'

'We haven't taken an official divorce yet. Why are you making it more difficult?'

'More difficult?' Swadha stopped in her tracks. 'Excuse me, stop behaving like a man-child. Men like you think their wife is their sponge. They would soak up whatever shit you throw at them. I'm making things easy for you, can't you see? Oh, how can I expect you to see anything when you never saw my love for you? So now, sit tight and relax. You don't have to breathe the same air as me.'

The doorbell rang. Swadha opened the door to usher in the security guard and asked him to take the luggage downstairs to her car.

'Message me when the papers are ready. I shall come and sign,' she said and followed the guard out. Haasil slumped on the couch—aghast—everything seemed to be collapsing around him. Palki had committed suicide, Swadha had left him and soon the police would find Palki's body and come for him on reading the note. Should he surrender? Haasil walked up to his bar, took out a bottle of Glenfiddich and kept gulping it down till his knees went weak.

* * *

Swadha had rented a place a few kilometres away from Haasil's. This was closer to her new office as well. After she had pulled all her luggage, one by one, into the flat, she ensconced herself on the sofa, huffing. It was a beautifully furnished flat. And neat. No tenant could have any complaint. But she did. The flat was empty of human beings. After years, she felt life had brought her back to the same loneliness that she used to feel when she lived alone in the city. The familiarity of the loneliness scared her. For she knew this one wasn't as comforting as before. This one had invisible canines that would bite her every second she was here. The most disturbing difference was that earlier, within the loneliness, she still had fantasies of the man she loved with her. Now those perfect fantasies had turned into ugly, blister-prone reality.

* * *

When after a couple of days, Haasil hadn't heard anything from the police or even read any news capsule regarding Palki's suicide, he pondered hard about the matter. He was expecting a call from the police as he had forgotten to take the suicide note with his name on it away. He was constantly toying with the idea of visiting the place again to talk to the landlord or the security guard to find out what had happened. Someone must have found the body. But he wasn't sure if it was the best time. The note only had his name. That wasn't really a deal-breaker for the police to contact him or accuse him per se. After all, he wasn't the only Haasil in the city. He was safe until his visiting the place was proved. He knew he was trapped in a Catch-22 situation.

It was when he was being driven through the traffic-laden Gurugram road that he received a video message on his phone from Palki's number. A deep frown appeared on his face as he quickly tapped and opened the video message.

Haasil broke into a cold sweat, sitting amidst the full blast of the car's air conditioning, seeing the video. He saw himself in the video discovering Palki's dead body, then hastily leaving the place. It brought forth three ugly truth bombs: one, Palki was probably murdered. Two, he was the potential prime suspect. Three, someone knew the first two truths.

Chapter 8

When the doorbell rang, Swadha thought it was the delivery guy from Swiggy. It had been a few days since she had started living in her new rented flat. She had officially left NH Consultants and joined the start-up. Work had kept her busy. And she was thankful for that. She had come home late that night and had ordered her dinner from the app. When she heard the doorbell, Swadha had freshened up by then.

It was Sanjana and Nitin standing with balloons, some soft toys, a cake and two bottles of champagne.

'You thought we would let you go without a housewarming party?' Nitin said. Looking at their happy, vibrant faces, Swadha realized how much she had been craving to smile. To just be happy without any reason. For if you want to be happy for a reason, life would make sure you remained happy only sparingly.

More food was ordered, more lights in the flat were switched on to take away the morose vibe while the champagne flowed freely. When Nitin excused himself to go to the washroom, Swadha opened up in front of Sanjana.

'I don't think I'll ever be able to forgive myself for what I did to my child,' she said, sounding choked.

'What has happened, has happened. You can't look at it as a wilful choice but as a circumstantial decision.'

'I wish execution was as easy as words,' Swadha said, wiping her tears and finishing her champagne.

While going back to their pad, Nitin was driving while Sanjana was lost in thought, looking out. He wanted to switch the music on but she had asked him not to.

'I still think they aren't done with each other,' Sanjana said.

'Me too.'

'But this staying away won't help either. Communication is the only medicine for any relationship woes.'

'You're right. I did have a talk with Haasil. He seems on a different trip itself. Sort of denial. Looked unusually anxious and yet didn't open up at all. So I couldn't even suggest anything.'

They drove on quietly. Then Nitin asked her something that made Sanjana uncomfortable.

'Did Swadha tell you what made them take this decision?'

After some quick introspection, Sanjana shook her head in the negative.

'I don't know.' And she wondered how in today's times one kept posting all the lovey-dovey pictures of their spouses on social media, wrote heartwarming captions to go with them, but when it came to important aspects of life, more often than not, many kept things to themselves. It didn't matter how much Nitin loved her or she loved him; he still didn't know that she had aborted their child. Maybe he would never know it. Likewise, maybe there were things that she didn't know about Nitin.

'Let's just do our best to get them together,' she said.

'Hmm, let me think of something.'

* * *

From the time Haasil had received the cam feed video, he didn't know what to think or do. The only thing he was sure of was that Palki had been murdered. And the fact that he was being blackmailed told him the murderer wanted to trap him. The simple conclusion was that perhaps Palki's murder was collateral, while cornering him probably was the principal agenda. But he couldn't be sure of it. It was all presumptions that would get cleared when the blackmailer asked something of him. That's why people blackmail. To demand either money or something important to them. But no such call for ransom or otherwise had come to him. Haasil did try to reach out to the number that had WhatsApped him but he reached a dead end with it. He did think of involving the police but then realized he would lose more than gain if he did so.

Finishing his drink, Haasil paid the bill and moved out. He intentionally hadn't called the driver that night. Though drunk but still feeling steady, he took the steering wheel. As he drove out of the parking lot, images of Palki's dead body kept flashing in front of his eyes. The alcohol made him press on the accelerator and then he had to abruptly brake. Someone had suddenly come in front of him.

Did he hit someone for real? Haasil quickly stepped out and saw a woman lying in front of the car. He wasn't sure if she had collapsed due to his car hitting her or the shock of the possibility of the car hitting her. He looked around.

There weren't many people around. But the ones who were there, were steadily approaching him. In no time it could turn into a hit-and-run case if he tried to get back into his car.

Clouded by alcohol, Haasil went and turned the woman lying on the road over. And he couldn't believe what he saw. It was Palki. Haasil was trying to get her back to consciousness, with soft slaps on her cheeks, by which time a few of the passersby had surrounded him.

'Is she alive?' asked one.

'You know her?' asked another, hearing him say the woman's name. Before the people could get involved, Haasil said aloud, 'Of course I know her. A friend. Let me take her to the hospital.'

Haasil drove away and then parked the car on the side of the road, switched the interior lights on and checked whether Palki had any external injuries. She didn't. There was no blood anywhere. Haasil relaxed. As he looked at Palki's face in the light up-close, it dawned on him that it wasn't Palki. It was . . .

'Pallavi?' Haasil frowned deeply as he murmured to himself in disbelief. Life had become one dramatic movie for him in the last few days. Should he take her to the hospital or . . . bringing in a hit-and-run case meant a lot of details would have to be provided and eventually would involve the police as well. Haasil decided to take her home. He would apologize for the almost-accident and ask her to leave once she gained consciousness.

Once home, Haasil took care to lay Pallavi down on the bed in the guest bedroom. He went out and drank some more from his bar. And didn't realize when he dozed off. It was around 3.30 a.m. when Pallavi opened her eyes. All through, the unconsciousness was a pretence. When she was confident

Haasil wasn't around, she got up and tiptoed outside to find him asleep on the couch.

Pallavi went close to him. It had been years since she had seen him from this close. She bent down to his slightly open mouth and inhaled the air he was exhaling. *Elixir!* Then she took her phone and clicked a selfie with her smiling and Haasil asleep. She sent it to Eerav with a message: *To new beginnings.*

Chapter 9

After sending Eerav the message, Pallavi brushed her lips as gently as she could on Haasil's forehead. Then she went to the bedroom, dug her face in the pillow and cried her heart out. At times like these she ceased to be the 'bitch' that the people she had toyed with—her colleagues, friends and, to an extent, her parents—knew her as. Only in that lonesome catharsis did Pallavi know her hard and snobby-bitch avatar was only a facade. It was her way to deal with her vulnerability, her weakness, her failure which Haasil, unknowingly, had exposed years back. In this lonesome moment, she aspired to be a girl with a sorted past, a simple present and a normal future. She didn't want to be different in any way but, deep within, she knew even though we are all born equal, our wounds give us an exclusivity. And in the exclusive persona her wounds had gifted her, Pallavi knew she had destroyed her true self. She slept with her tears drying on her pillow.

In the morning when Pallavi got up, she knew she had to pretend she was in slight pain and show disbelief in front of him on realizing she was, of all the people in the world, at Haasil's place. And she did the same seeing him sitting looking out from the deck. Haasil turned to see her standing there. He immediately apologized for accidentally hitting her and bringing her home without her permission. But he wasn't the only one who apologized.

'Perhaps this coincidence happened because I was craving it badly,' Pallavi said. She sounded guilty. 'I've been wanting to apologize for a long time for whatever happened in the past. I don't know whether you will understand or not but seeing my first love in front of me and an opportunity to get into his life, I had no choice but to accept what Nitin had offered back then. If I had known it would offend you, I would never have done it.'

In the silence that followed, Haasil now understood Pallavi better because in the last seven to eight years, he too had taken decisions and committed actions that were dictated by the situation he had found himself in. Prior to that, he had lived with the mistaken presumption that people were either black or white. But his marriage to Swadha and the subsequent connection with Palki taught him people could be of any colour at any given point in time depending on the situation. It's the give and take between the person and the situation which, in the end, defines his or her shade.

'It's okay. I guess all of us were pretty caught up with our own stories,' Haasil said.

'So, should I think you have forgiven me?' Pallavi sounded surprised. And saw him nodding.

'Thank you so much, Haasil. You just lifted a weight from my heart. Now I can die peacefully.'

'Why would you want to die when your entire life is in front of you?'

Pallavi was happy the conversation was going just as she had intended.

'Well, I don't have much to look forward to. Maybe I need a person who is as broken and hopeless as myself. And I don't think I will get him.'

Haasil felt she was talking more about his state than hers. She actually was. She chose her words wisely to subliminally convince him that she was the only one who could understand him in his current state. Pallavi didn't linger on for long and soon left. Not before keeping a tissue on the table beside him.

'This has my number. I know you may not want to get in touch again, but at least I would live with the hope that one day you may.' It was classic reverse psychology.

With Swadha negated and Palki gone from Haasil's life, Pallavi's plan was simple. Slowly manipulate Haasil's present emotional and vulnerable side and make a re-entry into his life. This time for forever. And finally live a life being her true self, busting the pretence of a mean bitch once and for all. And the accident—dropping in front of Haasil's car—was the first step towards that life. After she left, Haasil glanced at the tissue with her phone number. An impulse made him save the number on his phone.

Haasil had taken leave from office and was drinking alone sitting on the deck, when he got a call from Nitin.

'Sanjana has a surprise to share and you have to make it home later tonight,' Nitin said. Haasil tried to make some excuse but, on hearing Nitin's excitement, he guessed perhaps they were stepping into parenthood or something, and thus agreed. Little did he know it was only an excuse to get Haasil and Swadha together.

Later that night, a somewhat sober Haasil drove to Nitin's place. One look at Swadha sitting inside and he knew why the get-together was happening. Not that it pissed him off as much as Swadha, who was angry with Sanjana for pulling off such a prank.

Haasil stepped in. Neither did he initiate any conversation with Swadha, nor did she. Nitin took Haasil to the other corner of the room to talk to him while Swadha went inside the kitchen to join Sanjana.

'Just talk to her,' Nitin said.

'You think I didn't try?' Haasil countered.

'I know you did but you know how women are. It's your marriage, bro, a little bit of ego massaging won't mean much in the longer run but right now, it may end up saving the relationship.'

Haasil couldn't tell him exactly why Swadha was angry with him. That would mean he would have to tell him about Palki. A few silent seconds later, Nitin said, 'I don't think you have the right to be arrogant in this matter anyway.'

Haasil shot a sharp glance at him. *Did he know?*

'Why would you say that?'

'Don't tell Sanjana I ratted out but she too took her time to tell me this.'

'What?' Haasil couldn't wait.

'That Swadha told her it was all about this woman with whom you were having an affair.'

Haasil swallowed a lump in his throat, looking shell-shocked. *How the hell did Swadha know? He had never told her about Palki. He hadn't even mentioned an affair. Had she known it all along?* Haasil felt an impulse to talk to her then and there.

'Excuse me,' Haasil said and dashed towards the kitchen. He would have entered it had he not heard the rather loud voice of Swadha telling Sanjana that she would never forgive Haasil for turning her into a murderer. And things fell into place for Haasil, or so he thought, as he stood frozen outside the kitchen.

Does it mean it was Swadha who had killed Palki and was blackmailing him? Why else would she refer to herself as a murderer? Haasil was having a bad feeling right in his gut. And a raging anger.

Chapter 10

As Swadha headed out of the kitchen, she was taken aback seeing Haasil standing right at the door. One I-don't-give-a-damn-if-you've-eavesdropped glance, and she walked ahead. Haasıl wanted to stop her and inquire what exactly she meant but knew this wasn't the right time. He swallowed his inquisitiveness bordering on anger and carried on with the night.

It was when Swadha was booking an Uber after the party was over that Sanjana asked, 'What happened to your car?'

'Servicing,' she said.

'Let me drop you?' Haasil immediately proposed. Swadha was about to answer with a no when Sanjana grasped her hand tight. It was a gesture to stop her.

'I think that would be great,' Sanjana answered for her. Though Swadha gave her a sharp, accusing glance, she knew why Sanjana was vouching for it. They still thought conversation would lead to something meaningful, while Swadha had by now understood that the more she talked to Haasil, the more she would hate him. Sometimes it was better to terminate the connection at a point before which it turned absolutely ugly. Swadha knew they were both on the brink of such a point.

Half an hour later, Swadha found herself settling into Haasil's Maybach but she chose to sit behind the driver's seat. It was intentional. She had realized that, if one had to sever oneself from a person, one had to sever from the habits one had towards the person. If everything was normal, she would have sat right beside Haasil. If everything was normal . . . she left the train of thoughts midway, took her AirPods out and switched on her music at full blast. And that too was playing something they had once made love to. Swadha immediately stopped it, then played a genre which she loathed.

It was when an ad was playing in the music app that Swadha came back to the present. Till then she was lost god-knows-where. And she realized Haasil was driving on a road that wasn't familiar. She stopped the song.

'Where are we going?'

Haasil didn't respond. Swadha looked suspicious.

'Stop the car, Haasil.'

Taking an abrupt turn from the main road towards a service road, Haasil parked the car under a flyover. There was nobody around. Sounds of vehicles speeding over the flyover could be heard sporadically.

Swadha saw Haasil get down, keeping the car engine and headlights on. He came around the car to open Swadha's door. She shrugged at him, guessing something major was up.

'What I'm going to ask now, you better answer me truthfully without wasting my time,' he said.

Swadha frowned as Haasil asked, 'Did you kill Palki? Did you send me the cam feed video?'

Swadha had no clue what he was talking about.

'Are you drunk?'

'Fuck this innocence,' Haasil said. He had an aggressive pitch in his voice. He moved forward and held Swadha's throat with all his strength.

'I heard you tell Sanjana that I turned you into a murderer. And guess what, I know who the hell you have killed. So just cough out the truth.' Haasil seemed like a man possessed. With every second he was tightening his hold around Swadha's throat. For a moment she thought she was losing her senses. A countdown of sorts had begun in her mind and only when she almost reached the end of it did she feel Haasil's hand loosen up. She quickly freed herself and pushed him to move out of the car. A car went past, and she understood Haasil must have released his grip on seeing it coming. She got her breath back by the time the car disappeared from sight. Haasil turned to her with the same aggressive intent.

'Don't you dare touch me, Haasil,' she said, coughed a bit and then continued, 'Yes, it's true you turned me into a murderer. It's because of you that I had to kill our child.'

Haasil thought she was trying to steer away from her guilty self.

'Don't bullshit me. When were you pregnant?'

'The day you maritally raped me.'

Haasil swallowed a lump in his throat as his anger subsided a bit.

'You have to prove it.'

Swadha pushed past him and picked her phone up from the car's floor. She called Sanjana and put it on speaker.

'Didn't you come with me to abort my child?' Swadha asked directly.

'What happened?' Sanjana caught the catastrophe-tinge in her voice.

'Just answer me. Didn't you?'

'Yes, I did.'

'Do share the number with Haasil so he can talk to the doctor since he isn't believing me,' Swadha said and ended the call. She booked an Uber and waited with a constant shiver, keeping a safe distance from Haasil. After some time, the car arrived, Swadha climbed in and went away. Haasil screamed out loud and punched his car till his knuckles hurt. What had life come to? He screamed once again. But still felt miserable.

Haasil came home, drank some more and was woken up by the doorbell. The clock showed it was ten, but he couldn't guess if it was day or night. He stood up and drew apart the curtains. The sun's rays made him squint. He stood there, feeling the weakest he had ever felt. The doorbell called for his attention. He didn't care. When it rang for the third time, Haasil went and opened the door, looking disinterested. He was taken aback seeing Pallavi there.

'I'm sorry but I forgot my wallet here,' she said. The truth was she hadn't taken it the other day, hoping Haasil would find it and call her. When the call didn't come, she decided to drop in.

'Oh, okay. Please come in,' Haasil said. Pallavi entered and pretended to search for her wallet. She found it in the guest bedroom and came out.

'I'm sorry to bother you,' she said.

'It's okay.'

'You look dismal. I hope everything is okay.'

That was what Haasil didn't want to hear. He knew he was on the edge of an emotional landslide and questions like these were the push off the edge.

'You can tell me if you want,' Pallavi added and took a few small steps towards him. She reached him and sensed a restlessness in him. Immediately, she noticed tears in his eyes. She felt a knot in her stomach.

'Hey! You all right?' She held him. And that was it. He broke down in her arms. Like a baby. Pallavi remained quiet without interrupting him. When she felt his hold was loosening a bit, she held his face in her hands. They were so close that their breath was falling on each other's faces. Their eyes remained linked.

'I'm always there for you,' Pallavi said, brushing her lips on to his. The emotional vulnerability, the situational weakness, made Haasil respond instead of resisting.

* * *

Meanwhile, at Swadha's place, Sanjana was appalled on hearing about Haasil's behaviour the previous night.

'I think you should tell him clearly that you know he is having an affair. And that . . .' Sanjana spoke for a good minute, then realized Swadha was looking lost.

'Are you even listening?'

'Something struck me, which I didn't notice last night,' Swadha said.

'What?'

'He had said something that sounded like I had killed Palki.'

Sanjana couldn't hide her surprise.

'Palki? Why would he say so? She is dead,' Sanjana said. 'You sure you heard him right?'

'I think so.'

'Who was the woman he was having an affair with? Don't tell me it was Palki?'

'No, it's Pallavi,' Swadha said, sounding contradictory.

'What are you saying? Nitin would have known it.'

'You think I should ask Haasil about it?'

Sanjana nodded. 'Yeah, before it gets more complicated.'

Swadha had called Haasil twice but there was no answer. Curiosity made her visit his place. She pressed the doorbell once and waited but nobody opened it. Swadha used her thumbprint to unlock the digital lock on the main door and stepped in. She was heading towards the bedroom when she stopped, seeing a mobile phone lying casually on the couch. It wasn't Haasil's. She went to it and picked it up. The screen was lit as if someone had just used the phone and dropped it on the couch. Before it could self-lock itself, Swadha tapped on it. It opened up to something that made her shudder deep inside.

Chapter 11

Once Swadha came to a little normality after seeing what she had on the phone, she went towards the bedroom. She peeped in and saw Haasil lying on the bed with his eyes closed. He seemed naked beneath the blanket. There were female undergarments on the floor but no one else in sight. Then she heard the shower in the bathroom. Swadha went to the hall, shared what she saw on the phone to her WhatsApp, removed all proof of it and then, after placing the phone on the couch, left quietly.

Haasil had thought of giving office a miss. Pallavi had showered and prepared breakfast for them. She had slowly crept inside his space without him complaining about it. She was glad that the way she had to make Haasil vulnerable prior to this had paid off.

'This wasn't necessary,' said Haasil, seeing the breakfast.

'The least I could do to thank you,' Pallavi said, laying it out on the table.

'And don't worry, I won't be a liability. I will leave after this,' she added. Her role was to make Haasil feel as comfortable as possible in front of her. Only then would he crave her presence to escape the shit-storm that had hit him.

It was during the breakfast that Nitin called him. Haasil was in no mood to go to the office. But Nitin stated that an important client call had been set up. He reluctantly agreed. An hour later, Haasil entered his cabin only to see Swadha sitting beside Nitin.

'She has something to show you,' Nitin said. He sounded grim.

'What's this about?' Haasil said, taking a seat.

'Palki,' Swadha said. And handed her phone to him. Haasil noticed it was the same cam feed angle that had been sent to him when he had gone to meet Palki, only to discover her dead body. But in the cam feed video that he was watching, Haasil saw Palki—alive—sitting in a corner and weeping. She seemed to be in distress. The time stamp on it showed it was this morning's feed. Haasil's jaw had dropped by then.

It took him some time to narrate everything to both Swadha and Nitin since the day he had first spotted Palki until he found her dead and then the chance entry of Pallavi into his life. Both Nitin and Swadha were in shock.

'Couldn't you see the pattern? Two chance entries. One of Palki and one of Pallavi,' said Nitin.

Thinking back, Haasil realized Nitin made sense when he joined the two apparently mutually exclusive events. He intentionally didn't tell them about his recent moment-of-weakness episode with Pallavi.

'What do we do? Call the police?' Swadha asked.

'Any idea which place this could be?' Nitin turned to Haasil. The latter looked at the video where Palki had been seen again. And realized the room had the same curtains that Palki had at her place. Was she being held captive by Pallavi in her own place?

Haasil called Pallavi and in an unassuming manner asked her to meet up for lunch. Pallavi was overjoyed. She couldn't believe it was happening so fast. She made sure she gave Palki her food—sliding it in—and then dressed up for the lunch.

When Palki had woken up, after being made unconscious by Pallavi, she found herself locked inside a room which was soundproof. She banged on the door, called for Pallavi, for help, only to realize in the end her one trusted friend was the perpetrator. Pallavi didn't explain anything to her. She had only told her that she would make her unconscious before Haasil came so that things would look real. But Palki didn't realize that, by the time she woke up, an entire new story had taken place around her. Pallavi only kept supplying her food and other necessary items but kept her under strict house arrest. Palki fought against the close walls as much as she could but then resigned herself to her fate.

Dreams are achieved with hard work. But in Pallavi's case, reality had been manipulated to achieve her dream. Everything was just perfect. Seeing Haasil sit opposite her and have lunch was something she hadn't imagined. Though initially she had planned to destroy him, she was grateful for the moment when she saw the cam feed of Palki and him making love and decided to claim him instead. Once and for all.

As the lunch proceeded, Haasil excused himself to go to the washroom. Pallavi picked up her phone to casually check Palki's feed when she got the shock of her life on seeing Palki staring at the cam in the room. She had a sharp nail of sorts in her hand. Palki diabolically smiled at the cam and then poked the nail into her neck. It looked as if she had harmed herself in a fatal way. Pallavi couldn't believe her eyes. Anxiety gripped her. The moment Haasil came back, Pallavi gave him an excuse about work and hurried out. She didn't know Haasil was following her. And had intimated Swadha and Nitin by then.

As Pallavi reached her place, she quickly unlocked the door and went straight inside. She unlocked the bedroom door where Palki was and came in to see her lying on the floor. But there was no blood on or around her which would have surely squirted out, had she truly jabbed the nail in. Before she could check if Palki was alive, she heard the doorbell. Just like it had happened with Haasil. Nervous, she scampered out, leaving the bedroom door ajar.

Pallavi opened the main door to see Haasil, Nitin and Swadha there. A moment later, Palki appeared behind her. It was game over for her.

Yet again, the happiness that Pallavi thought was for forever turned out to be an illusion-bubble that had been busted.

Chapter 12

It was a Greek island-based theme café where Swadha and Palki met up. A little more than a month had gone by since they had caught the mischief-maker of their life. Everything had been clarified prior to their meeting. But a personal decision was yet to be made. Haasil didn't want to be a part of it. He too was guilty of pretence in front of Swadha since the night he had proposed to her. He was guilty of lying to Palki once as well. And now he thought he would accept whatever the ladies decided, with no words spoken even if it meant they wanted him out of their lives.

It was difficult for both Swadha and Palki. For the latter, even more because she was fighting her image of Haasil, her vague memories of him and the false information that Pallavi had fed her about him. There was no cloud-kitchen start-up or a restaurant, there were no loan sharks and there was no betrayal. The accident was just that. An unfortunate event. But what that one chance event had triggered in their lives was what they had wrestled with for years now in their own ways. And had brought them to this point where all three—Swadha, Haasil and Palki—had to make life-altering decisions.

It was Swadha who initiated the talk on the subject after the ladies had ordered their coffee and chit-chatted for some time.

'I thought about it a lot. We both have two options. Either to be with Haasil or to leave him. Well, I can only talk about myself. When I started thinking about the options, I realized there wasn't any option, really. If he stays with you, he won't ever think of me. But with me, he will always think of you. So it's only natural that I should step back here. Most importantly, for myself. Being married to Haasil was anyway a dream. The last seven or eight years we had were like an action-packed movie. I learnt so much about life, about myself.'

Palki smiled and said, 'Couldn't be more action-packed than mine.'

Swadha returned her smile. She liked Palki's vibe. It was soothing.

Palki continued, 'I was waiting for you to tell me what you have decided. Mine would be based on that. But the one thing I would have anyway said is, I'm really sorry for the loss of your child.'

Swadha took a deep breath.

'I think it would be the one episode in my life which I'll never be able to move on from. Guess we all have that one thing that torments us for life.'

Palki nodded. A few silent moments passed by.

'You must have hated me, right, when you got to know Haasil was married to me?' Swadha asked.

'Only as much as you are hating me right now.'

Both women burst out laughing. From some distance, Haasil was watching them. Seeing them laugh, he hoped things finally would turn out good. But a nervousness was still fluttering within him. Sometime later he saw them get up, hug and then Swadha left.

Palki strolled towards him. Haasil stood with bated breath as if life was about to announce where he would have to go. To hell, or to heaven.

'She said she would happily sign the divorce papers. And she has wished us luck.'

Haasil hugged Palki tight. He could hear his own heart beat hard. He did think about it many times but could never imagine how he would live if Swadha had chosen otherwise. For he wouldn't have fought it. His respect for Swadha escalated manifold. Breaking the hug, Palki said, 'I'm glad our love story worked out eventually.'

Haasil gave her a wide smile.

'This eventuality took its own not-so-sweet time. And I swear I still don't believe we've made it.'

The two climbed into his Maybach and drove off together.

Epilogue

The wedding was to take place in three hours' time. Everyone in Eerav's family was busy. The hubbub was of a typical Delhiite wedding with songs, liquor and dance happening at the drop of a hat. Everyone was smiling. Except for the groom himself. Eerav was in his room. After he received a voice note from Pallavi, he asked every friend of his to get out of his room. And then he played it. Her voice sounded different.

Dear human diary,

Imagine you've been having a headache since your teens. One that never subsides. You can't tell this to anyone because it can't be seen or caught in any medical test but only felt. When it lasts for a certain time, it actually begins to isolate you from yourself. And one day at a time, it kills you by making you believe that you deserve the headache. Love has been one such headache for me. But now I've finally understood love isn't for me. The person love made me is someone I can do without. I harmed more people being in love.

And that's not how love needs to be expressed. But being rejected by Haasil, I never knew of any other way of using love than to destroy first myself and then him. Eventually, my silly self-created hatred-bubble has been busted. It's a myth that when hatred ceases to exist, love appears. Love is always there. But now I know when hatred stops, sense appears. You understand things the way you should.

Though I didn't actually lie the last time we met that I was trying to focus on myself, I made a blunder again by choosing a wrong way to create that core. I tried manipulating people again to suit my needs. Perhaps that's my core. I have the skill to actually convince people of many things. Except I couldn't convince myself of one simple fact: Haasil isn't made for me. But what do you do when your love is innocent but your desires are dark? I guess, you become a 'Pallavi'.

You know, once Haasil, Swadha and Palki busted my plan, what hurt me the most? That they didn't do the obvious. They didn't press any charges against me. Didn't hand me over to the police for forcefully keeping Palki captive or misleading her about Haasil. They simply let me go, let me be. I know why they must have done it. Out of sympathy. It broke me. A spirit like mine thrives on challenges. If they had registered an FIR against me, then it would have been a challenge. I would have fought them. But they forgave me. What do you do when someone forgives you? There can't be any fight against forgiveness. It made me realize how unimportant and frivolous I was for people whose lives I was manipulating, about whom I was thinking day and night, who had become the epicentre of my life again in the last few years. Haasil Sinha doesn't belong to me. Period. I've accepted it. But like all acceptance, mine too needed a journey to discover it. A journey where I broke several times, was moulded by life to become this bitch that I'm known as amidst people who think they know me.

Remember that drunk walk on the highway I made you do to test if we could become each other's human diaries? Now I'm doing the same test on myself again after I send this voice note. When you hear this voice note, the result of the test would be out. Will I survive to give life another chance or will I die to finish this pitiful existence . . . I don't know. Let me find out.

The moment the voice note ended, Eerav immediately called her. His gut was telling him something bad had already happened. But he was praying it was just an empty feeling. The more it rang, the faster he found his heart racing. Till the call was picked up.

'Pallavi, you there?'

'Of course,' came her voice.

'Your voice note scared the fuck out of me. You all right?'

'Pallavi can destroy herself for a man, but she can never kill herself for a man. Don't worry, I'm all right, my human diary. Just a little lighter now. By the way, now that I'm alive, I'm coming to your wedding. Ask the men to be on their highest alert.'

Acknowledgements

The main motivation for writing this book are my readers who appreciated its predecessor, *That Kiss in the Rain*. It was published almost thirteen years ago. The fact that I'm penning its sequel after so many years tells me the characters of Pallavi, Haasil, Palki and Swadha nested somewhere deep within the ones who read it. Deep gratitude for that. I hope you like the sequel as well. This also happens to be my first unplanned sequel to any of my previous works. That way, it's special.

Heartfelt thanks and gratitude to:

Milee Ashwarya—Can't thank you enough for being the constant source of inspiration and motivation.

Vijesh Kumar—Thanks for all the prompt action and the support you show for my books.

Ralph Rebello—for the smooth copy-edits. It was a pleasure working with you on another book.

The entire marketing team at Penguin Random House India for their constant support.

Ranisa—Rather 'Mommy-sa' now. So happy for your new innings. I'm sure you're going to be a rock star mother. Best wishes always.

Friends and family—for being there whenever I need you all.

R—for everything, all the time!